CW00530747

The Berlin Family's Secret

Baruch Cohen

Producer & International Distributor
eBookPro Publishing
www.ebook-pro.com

The Berlin Family's Secret
Baruch Cohen

Translation: Ruth Cohen Korabelnik
Contact: ruthyck@gmail.com
ISBN 9789655754124

The Berlin Family's Secret:

A Historical WW2 Novel

Baruch Cohen

Preface

After World War II, while I was active in the illegal immigration to the Land of Israel, I witnessed the survivors of the Holocaust with my own eyes, broken shells of men and women, who had just come out of hell. I dedicate this book to them.

Baruch (Boby) Cohen, Yavne

Translator's Note

Growing up on the appreciation of Jewish history, I feel that it was part of my father's legacy to disseminate the events recounted in this book to future generations, for them to learn and understand the importance of avoiding another Shoah (Holocaust) at all costs.

Ruth Cohen Korabelnik
Yavne, Israel 2023

Table of Contents

Happiness and its Shards 9
Five Minutes to Barbarossa 35
Fall of the Heroes 101
Buchenwald 191
Berlin in Flames 227
Epilogue 241

Happiness and its Shards

1

Marlene Kerner lived in a state of fear.

At the Opera Place, right in the center of town, a public ceremony of burning Jewish books was being held. Students, professors, and government ministers gathered to participate. The speakers at the ceremony likened the Jews to contagious bacteria, and discussed the necessity of cleansing the atmosphere from them.

Shortly after they started burning books, the Germans began burning down synagogues. Almost every day, the newspapers published new measures imposed on the Jewish population, further restricting their civil liberties. In Berlin, for example, the licenses of Jewish lawyers were revoked, even of those who worked in the public service.

Franz, Marlene's husband, tried to comfort her.

"No one knows that you're Jewish, not even the children, and they are usually the first to talk."

He didn't tell her about the publications he has been receiving at his pharmacy on Friedrichstrasse, from universities and various cultural institutes, which were laden with poisonous attacks against the Jews. All he wanted was to preserve the lifestyle they enjoyed, that of a typical, upper-middle-class German family, living in the nation's capital.

Franz educated his and Marlene's three children—Karl, the eldest; Elsa, two years his junior; and Helmut, the youngest—in the spirit of devotion to their motherland, Germany. But over time, he started questioning whether the events that have been taking place in their beloved country since the rise of Hitler, were actually in its benefit.

In the beginning of 1933, restrictions were imposed on Berlin's Jews with regards to economy, culture and arts. The racist Nuremberg Laws, enacted two years later, validated those restrictions.

At the time, the family was still living a relatively comfortable life. While Franz was aware of the fact that intellectual groups in the country's main universities—Berlin, Frankfurt, Breslau, Freiburg, and others—were publishing venomous anti-Jewish articles, only in late 1938 did he understand how deeply everything had changed.

On November 7th, 1938, a Jewish man named Herschel Grynszpan assassinated Ernst vom Rath, the third secretary of the German Embassy in Paris. As a result, anti-Jewish riots broke out overnight throughout Germany. That night became known as Kristallnacht (Crystal Night, or the Night of Broken Glass). 700 synagogues were set on fire and Jewish businesses were nationalized by the authorities. 1000 Jews were brutally murdered, and some 25,000 were deported to concentration camps such as Buchenwald and Sachsenhausen. Adding insult to injury, Jews were fined one billion dollars for damages caused by the riots.

Speaking at the Reichstag on January 30th,1939—less than three months later—Hitler proclaimed that "If the international financial Jewry will stall the war in Europe, the result will not be its victory, but rather, the total destruction of the Jewish race."

Franz saw the hatred of those wearing the SA shirts, the ongoing persecution and the steep decline in Berlin's Jewish population in 1939 alone, from 120,000 to a mere 91,000. Jews

were no longer allowed to live in certain neighborhoods or use public transportation, and were placed under nighttime curfew, from 8 pm until 8 am. Through the publications he received at his pharmacy, Franz learned about *Lebensraum*, the need for more land for the "master race", the Germans.

Franz started weighing his options, calmly and slowly—as if he were reviewing the individual ingredients of a medicine he prepared in his pharmacy. Eventually, he concluded that Germany's Jewish population had become the target of dangerous hatred, and that his wife had every reason to be worried: for herself, for their children and for him as well.

If Marlene hadn't gotten sick with bone cancer that same year, perhaps Franz would have done something. But his feelings of concern, sympathy and pity for his suffering wife pushed aside his growing aversion to the regime's actions. In April 1940, Franz buried his Jewish wife, in a Catholic cemetery in Berlin, under a beautiful tombstone. Next to the grave he planted a lilac bush, Marlene's favorite flower.

After his beloved wife passed away, Franz went through a period of deep crisis. While he loved Marlene with all of his heart, it was more than her mere death that devastated him: it was the fact that he buried her in a Christian cemetery. He knew that he should have buried her in a Jewish one, but his fear for his children's fate, lest it be known their mother was Jewish, made him bury her as a "true" Christian.

Marlene's parents immigrated to Frankfurt from Warsaw in the early 1900s. Life in Poland at the time was very difficult. Jews were persecuted and endured terrible pogroms. The lucky ones managed to immigrate to the New World, to the USA while

others, like Marlene's parents, moved to the Western lands of Europe.

The period in which the Wilczek family emigrated from Warsaw to Frankfurt bore regime changes and a hostile attitude towards Europe's Jews, largely due to the continent's economic crisis. Unemployment and hunger were rampant. Marlene's father, Frank Wilczek, was a sickly man who struggled to find work and her mother, Vera, did all sorts of petty jobs. Alex, her brother, managed to find employment in a food company, and received his pay either in food or in food stamps, which helped ease the hunger at home. He worked there during his teenage years, until he was drafted to the German military towards the end of the Great War.

Franz met Marlene in 1921. It was his last year in the pharmaceutical faculty of the University of Frankfurt. One night, he went out with his friends to the Melody Club—one of the city's most popular clubs at the time. Marlene was one of the many girls he met there, and she immediately captured his attention. She was very beautiful, with deep blue eyes and blond hair, which she wore in a contemporary style. Franz thought they would only flirt with each other that one night, without any serious outcome.

However, they saw each other again. Their third meeting already took place at his university dorm room, where he gently took her to his bed, lay her down, and tenderly kissed her lips. She willfully responded and groaned as he slipped his hand under her blouse. She took the blouse off and there they were— two beautiful, alabaster, pear-like breasts.

As Franz moved his hand towards them, Marlene stopped him and quietly asked:

"Aren't you afraid of having sex with a Jewish girl?"

But Franz was too aroused by her gorgeous body to even reply. He covered her with kisses and they made love.

That was the night Marlene lost her virginity. Afterwards, she asked him again:

"Aren't you afraid of having sex with a Jewish girl?"

"I am not acting in haste or being irrational," Franz replied in his normal, even tone. "I am sure that our connection will lead to something good."

Marlene looked at him silently. He suddenly realized this wasn't the answer she had expected from him. But then he added another sentence, which surprised them both:

"Marlene, I want you to be my wife."

Marlene told her brother, Alex, about how much she loved Franz, and about his rapid proposal. Alex was happy for her and urged her to agree, adding that she shouldn't look back on where she had come from, but rather follow her fate. Alex also delivered the message to their parents: he told them that their daughter is engaged to a scholar with a good profession, and while he is not Jewish, he loves her with all of his heart and will provide for her with a good living.

Franz was madly in love with Marlene, with her beauty, her tenderness and her serenity. At the time, there was no taboo on Christians marrying Jews. Yet, the couple decided to conceal this fact from Franz's parents and friends, just as a precautionary measure. The parents on both sides were happy about the upcoming union and gave their blessing.

Following Franz's internship, his parents helped him open up his very own pharmacy. A short while after that, Franz and Marlene were married, and in 1922 already welcomed their first child, Karl. Two years later Elsa was born, followed by Helmut, the youngest, the year after.

The pharmacy prospered, and the Kerners were well-off and had no financial concerns. The children played with those of their neighbors, the Fröhlichs. Mr. Fröhlich was 55 years old, and a great supporter of the new regime. Karl, Elsa and Helmut also enjoyed playing with the children of their other neighbors, the Keitel family. No one on their street knew if there was truth to the rumors that they were related to General Wilhelm Keitel, the Supreme Commander of the Armed Forces. However, once a month, a luxurious car adorned with a prominent swastika and the Nazi flag, stopped by their home. While Franz never spoke a word to anyone in that family, he still allowed his children to play with theirs.

After Marlene's death, the Kerner home, once so warm and welcoming, became the dwelling of sadness. It was very difficult for Franz to open the pharmacy every morning and concentrate on his work. He blamed himself for being inattentive to his wife's condition. "If only had I taken her to the best doctors, we might have discovered the damned disease earlier," he said to Karl.

"How could you have even known she was sick? Mother never complained," Karl pointed out.

"I should have thought about it, about your mother's health," replied Franz.

Meanwhile, Karl's recruitment day was approaching, which worsened Franz's mood even more. He did not discuss the concerns he had with his children, but kept asking himself about

his son's potential fate: Where would he do his training? Where would he serve, in Germany or in one of the lands it had occupied? And—for God's sake— would he live, or would he die?!

2

Herbert and Rosie Kerner had two sons: Franz, the eldest, born in 1900, and Ditmar, two years his junior. The boys were very similar except for one thing: Franz was blond-haired with a light complexion, whereas Ditmar was dark. This influenced his course of life. Ever since his childhood, when his father nicknamed him der Schwarze (the black one), Ditmar felt he had to prove that he was just as Aryan as his older brother.

After graduating from high school with distinction, Ditmar enrolled into law school at the prestigious University of Berlin. His parents helped with the tuition, and he also gave private lessons in chemistry and math to support himself.

When Franz returned home with his future wife, Marlene, Ditmar was almost 20 years old. He felt an awkward sense of jealousy towards his brother, who had already completed his studies and was about to marry a beautiful young woman and start his own pharmacy, with their parents' help.

As the years went by, the relationship between the brothers worsened. What started as sibling rivalry soon glided over to the political sphere, mainly because Ditmar, during his senior year of university, joined the Association of Young Lawyers for the Nation. This association was established by the National Party, and its main goals were abolishing the Treaty of Versailles and expelling all Jews from government offices.

Following his graduation, Ditmar found a job at a large, well-known Berlin law firm, named Heckel and Schultz. He started as an apprentice, and two years later became an associate and began working on important, challenging cases.

In 1933, four months after the Nazi Party rose to power, Ditmar received a claim against a wealthy Jewish carpet manufacturer named Grünfeld. The man's factory was completely burnt down by unknown vandals, and he sued his insurance company for 250,000 Reichsmarks. Ditmar represented the insurance company, which was eventually fully exempt from paying anything at all. Furthermore, the Jewish man was blamed for the fire, and accused of burning down his own factory in order to receive the insurance compensation. He was sentenced to six months in prison and to a 100,000 mark fine. He had to sell his house and assets in order to gather this sum.

During a party at the end of 1935, Ditmar met Martha von Ringel, a beautiful 25-year-old member of the German nobility. Her father, Jürgen von Ringel, served Kaiser Wilhelm II in 1900. For this, the Kaiser had bestowed upon him the title *Graf* (count) and added the prefix "von" to his name.

Ditmar and Martha started seeing each other on a regular basis. They were invited to cocktail parties at the homes of Berlin's new financial elite, and frequented concerts and literature circles, where the new ideas of the Nazi ideology were presented and discussed. Their relationship was based on physical attraction, but Ditmar also greatly benefited from meeting so many high-ranking people, with key positions in the new regime. The following year, in 1936, Ditmar proposed to Martha, who gladly accepted.

Ditmar went to see his brother, Franz, in order to give him the wedding invitation. But the evening became heated as they began discussing the new Nuremberg Laws. Ditmar did not stop praising the Nazi regime, and Franz felt he was losing his mind.

"Have you seen the new laws against the Jews?"

"Until the rise to power of our Führer, the Jews took over our economy and culture. It's about time they are restricted," replied Ditmar.

"This isn't about restriction, this is complete annihilation!" cried Franz. "In Berlin, they are already breaking their skulls."

"I can't believe my ears!" raged Ditmar against his brother in his venomous tone, the one he reserved for political disputes. "Are you supporting them? I believed you and I shared the same notions. I must have been mistaken. You should know that your way of thinking is completely against German values and ideology."

"You are too influenced by the circles you attend!" reprimanded Franz. "I think you should reconsider this marriage."

Ditmar left his brother's house in a fury.

If it weren't for Franz's parents, he and Marlene would not have gone to the wedding.

As they had expected, the atmosphere at the wedding was polite but icy—as icy as Franz's heart, which he felt freeze in his chest upon seeing the new social elites from the courts, industries and universities, all Nazi supporters, along with top military officers, some in their uniforms and others wearing tuxedos.

Franz was stunned to see his brother's social circle. Their relationship was severed for many years to come.

3

Franz Kerner was feeling very miserable, sitting alone in his Berlin pharmacy, in the fall of 1940. At the time, Germany's political situation was very good; the previous year, the Germans had invaded Poland. The Wehrmacht only needed four and a half weeks to wipe out the Polish army, which was equipped with old weapons and armory. Poland became just another county in the expanding German empire. Russia, its neighbor to the east, conquered the region in Poland adjacent to the border, and at the same time signed a coexistence treaty with Germany. France was forced into signing a humiliating surrender agreement in Compiègne—ironically, in the same railway wagon where Germany had signed its own surrender in 1918.

The highly circulated newspaper, *Völkischer Beobachter*, provided a detailed description of the ceremony commemorating the arrival of the Führer in Compiègne. Hitler paused for a moment in front of the Glade of the Armistice and read the inscription: "Here, on the eleventh of November 1918 succumbed the criminal pride of the German empire... Vanquished by the free peoples which it tried to enslave."

Not a single muscle moved in the Führer's face, but he had a victorious spark in his eyes. He entered the wagon where the French representatives were awaiting.

The German citizens rejoiced in the streets, and victory celebrations lasted for several days and nights. But in contrast to his nation's happiness, Franz was incredibly sad, for he carried the heavy burden of his wife's secret. The most difficult thing for him was not telling his children.

Should I tell them the secret now, or continue concealing it? He kept wondering to himself.

Either option would have the potential of evoking future problems. Those thoughts haunted him constantly. His first concern was the welfare of his children. He was worried that if they found out about their ethnic origin, they would have to cope with unpleasant reactions from their friends and colleagues. Meanwhile, the entire nation was dragged along by the regime, which blamed the Jewish race for all the troubles in the world.

Franz was aware of everything. Deep down in his heart he disagreed with the hostile winds blowing against the Jews. Slowly-slowly, he felt how he was growing to resent the Nazi regime—this, while his eldest son, seventeen-and-a-half-year-old Karl, was already making plans to join the Garman Air Force, and his two younger children, Elsa and Helmut, were greatly enjoying their activity in the German youth movement, the *Hitlerjugend*.

As he sat alone, quietly, tormented by his thoughts, the beautiful face of his beloved late wife, Marlene, appeared to him. Franz concentrated on her memory for a long time, until he felt his heart grow stronger, and then made his decision: he will never tell his children that their mother was Jewish. That was the only way to guarantee them life.

4

In January of 1941, Karl completed his aviation course and was certified as a navigator at the Messerschmitt Bf109 aircraft, the backbone of the German Luftwaffe at the time. Karl took great pride in his uniform and the rank of second lieutenant he was awarded. During his short leaves at home, he would tell his father, sister and brother about the successful military operations in which he took part.

Franz noticed Karl's great pride, and while he made sure to praise him, his heart was broken. Karl's brother, Helmut, as well as his high school friends, admired him and hoped to follow in his footsteps.

But not long after, Karl returned home in a very somber mood, after having participated in the aerial attacks over the English city of Coventry. Karl was one of 400 pilots who took part in the strikes and luckily, returned safely to his base. But he was completely depressed. His father tried to get him to speak, but in vain.

The next morning, during breakfast, Karl was deep in thought. Only later that day did he start speaking about what he had gone through.

Karl recounted what he had seen during the attacks, how the skies of Coventry turned red as a result of the fires caused by the massive bombardment. This was the first time Karl witnessed, firsthand, what a combat plane can do to a civilian population. Radio London reported that 500 people were killed and more than 1000 were injured. Karl was having doubts whether this entire operation was even necessary, especially after realizing that more than 250 German pilots and crew members were also killed.

A few days later, Karl said goodbye to his family and headed again for the front, not sure he would ever see them again.

The following month, after another operation over the skies of Britain, Karl returned to his temporary base, near the French city of Rouen, and asked his commander for a 72-hour leave. Normally, after a full month of aerial warfare, pilots were allowed to submit a request and get few days off. This time, though, his commander was about to refuse his request because so much was planned for the coming days. However, upon noticing Karl's face, he understood how badly his subordinate needed that leave.

In the shower that night, Karl felt all the muscles in his body ache, the result of him sitting hunched over in the jet for so many hours. His heart ached as well. Karl realized just how lucky he had been: 80 German aircrafts and more than 100 pilots and crew members—almost half the force that participated in the mission—were shot down. Among those who perished were two of his best friends, Hans and Johan. Karl grieved for them deeply, and knew that this might be his own fate the next time.

On the train on the way home, Karl tried to get some sleep, but in vain. His deceased friends' faces kept appearing before him. When he arrived at his home, his father immediately knew something was wrong, and gave him a big hug. At that moment, Karl burst into tears. Franz held him tight, just like when he was a little boy, patting his shoulder and encouraging him to relieve his emotional burden.

Karl calmed down, took a sip of water, and started speaking:

"My good friends, Hans and Johan, were shot down over London. One moment I saw Johan flying next to me in the same flight formation, and the next, he disappeared. I assume he was shot down by an anti-aircraft missile."

Karl lowered his eyes and continued.

"Hans disappeared from the radar. That's what they told us in the post-mortem briefing. Apparently, he was also shot down by a missile," Karl was now sobbing again. "I feel so bad for them, they both had plans to study at the University of Berlin after the war. I am so frustrated and angry. Why were they killed, for God's sake? Why?!"

As Karl buried his face in his hands, Franz looked at him with compassion.

"You see, father, I could have been one of them," Karl cried out loudly.

Franz leaned over, put his hand on his son's shoulder and said, "This is the meaning of war. No one has an insurance policy. I wish I could tell you something different."

"I have to see their parents, they probably need support," Karl said, wiping his eyes.

The families of Karl's two friends lived in Nuremberg, which was considered the cradle of Nazism, alongside Munich. He took the 7:30 am train and five hours later, when he arrived, he realized that the buildings looked just like all the other ones throughout Germany. Nazi flags and signs with swastikas were hanging everywhere. Pictures of Hitler and other regime leaders were attached to house facades. Karl caught the tram to the city stadium, where Hans' family lived.

Hans' mother opened the door, recognized Karl immediately and gave him a warm hug.

"What are you doing here in Nuremberg?" she asked, surprised, but then suddenly realized something was terribly wrong. She collapsed onto the chair, speechless, and started crying:

"I had a wonderful son and now he is gone! I gave him to our country!"

She was trying to restrain herself. "Johan's father came to visit us two days ago, and told me that his son was shot down over London. I hoped Hans didn't go on that mission. They both will have their names written in gold letters in Germany's book of heroes."

It seemed she had reconciled with her fate. Han's father, who joined them in the living room, said: "Don't tell me anything else, I don't want to know, it doesn't matter anymore. I don't want to know what happened. Let him rest in peace."

Karl did not continue to Johan's parents; distress and sorrow filled his heart, and the emotional burden was almost too much to bear.

Karl's squadron was relocated to a different base, near Saarbrücken. It was very difficult for him. He felt the void left by his two late friends, and greatly missed their laughter and lewd jokes. Up in the air he was completely focused, but on the ground, he was absent-minded.

On one of the first days of May 1941, technicians arrived at the base in order to improve the shooting abilities of his aircraft. Karl stepped into the plane to admire their work, but as he got out, he didn't notice the service cart right behind him. The cart driver didn't notice him either, and accidentally ran over his right leg. Karl fell backwards, crying in pain. A car drove him to the clinic, with his ankle swelling and turning purple.

He limped inside, barely noticing the nurse who was busy taking care of another soldier. The doctor called him into his office, checked his ankle and wrote a note for the nurse on what should be done—the ankle required a light massage and then bandaging.

Karl gave the note to the nurse. As she lifted her eyes, he was stunned to see that it was none other than Eva, his high school sweetheart. They had been a couple all through their studies in Berlin, until he was drafted. She seemed all grown up, but remained as beautiful as he remembered her.

"Eva, what are you doing here?" He asked.

"I can't believe it!" she yelled excitedly. "The handsome Karl Kerner is now a pilot!"

The soldier she had just treated buttoned his shirt and left the room, leaving the two of them alone.

"I joined the military efforts of our country. I'm on duty now, and it's a long story," Eva said.

"Let's meet tonight, after your shift," suggested Karl.

"Not before I treat you according to the doctor's instructions," said Eva with a laugh. She began massaging his leg, and her touch already made him feel much better. She washed her hands and said with a smile: "My shift is over at six o'clock and I'll be free then."

At ten past six, Eva was waiting for Karl outside the clinic, wearing her uniform and sergeant tags on her shoulders. Karl approached her, took her by the arm and they began strolling

leisurely, telling each other their stories since the last time they had seen each other.

"After you left, I was seeing a young man who proposed to me. He thought that he would join the army while I remained home, pregnant and pining for him. I said 'No, thank you.' He was drafted, and I graduated nursing school and enlisted. I wanted to go as far as possible in order to forget him. That's how I made it here, to Saarbrücken," Eva concluded her story.

"And what about you?" She asked.

"I completed my aviation course about six months ago, but it feels like centuries had already passed," Karl said.

"Why?" asked Eva.

"Because I participated in too many air battles," Karl replied.

He took a long pause and then continued.

"We don't know what the future has in store for us". Eva looked at him, with fear in her eyes.

They continued strolling and passed by a bulletin board, on which hung a stylized, handwritten advertisement announcing a ball that was to be held that very night at the officer's club. They decided to go in, and enjoyed dancing to the piano music there. Someone explained that the piano was confiscated from the home of a foreign citizen. They all raised their glasses to their squadron's success and at midnight, they left the club, walking into the darkness.

Karl accompanied Eva to her quarters. She held onto his arm, so she wouldn't stumble in the dark. When they arrived at her doorstep, Karl hugged her, searching for her lips with his.

"Can you believe that out of all our schoolmates, it's me you ended up meeting, 500 kilometers away from home and during the war?" Karl asked.

"Not in my dreams," Eva replied, laughing.

Suddenly, Eva realized that Karl's face became streaked with sorrow. "What is this?" she asked, to which he replied, "You can't even imagine what I have been through."

"Please tell me," she asked of him, linking her arm through his.

"I lost my best friends, Hans and Johan. They were killed on mission during the attacks on London. Now they are fish food," Karl answered sadly.

They stayed together for ten more minutes, reminiscing about their beloved hometown, Berlin, and trying to dim the pain they both felt. They promised to meet again when the circumstances allow. Karl kissed her at length, a gentle kiss, and left not knowing when those circumstances would take place, if ever.

Five Minutes to Barbarossa

5

May and June of 1941 were months of rehabilitation and restoration for the German ground and air forces, which endured severe losses during the battle over Britain. The navy, too, was undergoing changes and urgently required additional staffing. This corps held the brunt of the military effort against the British navy in the North Sea and the Atlantic Ocean.

On June 20th, without prior warning, almost all of the German pilots who were stationed in western Germany and along the Rhine River, were relocated to the new Polish-German border. Karl's squadron also received the relocation order. He had very little time to deliver a message to his father, saying that he will now be stationed over the Polish border.

He flew his plane to the new base near Lublin, east of Warsaw. Upon landing, he was surprised to see a great deal of activity on the ground: infantry forces, tanks and German artillery were training along the border line. Karl wondered about this but no one, not even the veteran soldiers on the base, knew what was going on.

The next day, June 21st, the base commander called the pilots and the ground staff to deliver an important message. No one had any idea what he would say, and the atmosphere was tense. They all stood silently, and the commander announced:

"Our Führer decided that Germany will now launch Operation Barbarossa. Its main goal is to expel the Slavic people, the inferior race, beyond the Ural Mountains, because they can no longer continue living in Aryan Europe. In order to achieve this goal and guarantee the Wehrmacht's overwhelming victory—

utmost dedication, even self-sacrifice is required of each and every one of you. We hope that by New Year's Eve, this will all be behind us, and that we will celebrate the holiday at home."

The soldiers applauded enthusiastically. They were laughing and hugging each other, speaking in loud voices, happy and excited.

"Quiet!" The commander raised his voice. "Along the current border between us and the Bolsheviks, from the Baltic Sea to the Black Sea, the Wehrmacht is ready to fulfil its duty with the help of its allies: the Romanians, the Hungarians and the Finns. We are already moving forces on the ground, but we explained to the Russians that these were only local military maneuvers. The stupid Russians accepted our explanations. However, you must keep this information top secret, because surprise is our ultimate weapon. You are not allowed to say a word even to your families. Tonight, we will let you know your missions. May God be with you, Hitler's soldiers."

Everyone applauded again, so loudly it felt as if the hall was shaking. Karl and his friends were flabbergasted by the dramatic announcement. They understood something big was about to take place, but didn't realize just how soon.

The next morning, June 22nd 1941, at 4 am, Operation Barbarossa began.

In an unprecedented attack, massive German forces on the border began bombarding USSR territories. Karl's squadron, number 219, set out to attack airports, power stations, industrial plants and highways. They were ordered by their commanders to drop any remaining bombs they might have on centers of populations, in order to chase the Communists eastward.

The pilots successfully executed their first mission on the Soviet Front. They returned to the base without any losses and with no bombs left. On that first day, the massive ground invasion also began. More than 6 million soldiers, mostly Germans but also Romanians, Finns and Hungarians, marched into the Soviet Union, in the largest and greatest military invasion in human history.

The Russians, as well as all of Europe, were caught by complete surprise. Within six hours, massive Soviet forces were captured, and over the next few days that number reached almost 400,000. The streets filled with people trying to escape.

Hitler's forecast, that his soldiers would celebrate the coming Christmas at home, was about to come true.

On the seventh day of the invasion, Karl's squadron was placed under the command of the Central Front, headed by Field Marshal von Bock, one of the Wehrmacht's most esteemed commanders.

In August, Karl and three of his friends were promoted to captains. They were very proud, and invited all of their co-pilots for a celebratory drink.

In September, Karl's squadron received the Führer's announcement, that Soviet resistance on the Central European Front was collapsing. The crucial battle—the attempt to invade Moscow, the Soviet capital—was about to begin. By then, Karl's squadron had already lost a quarter of its men. For three months they were fighting ferociously, losing friends who were then rapidly replaced by new, unexperienced pilots. They were completely burnt out, and hardly had a moment to sleep, eat, or grieve for their fallen friends.

The new pilots told them that they were only taught the basics during their training, and were assured they would learn everything else during the battles. That assumption was obviously wrong, but who would dare resist the Führer and his commanders' demands?

The pilots were allowed to write short postcards home, disclosing nothing regarding their whereabouts.

In October, the first snow fell over the plains around Moscow. In two months, it would be Christmas, but the soldiers were no longer sure whether they would celebrate that holiday at home, as the Führer had promised. In fact, they weren't even sure whether they would celebrate any holiday in the future, at all.

6

A few months earlier, in February 1941, when Karl was still flying over Britain and bombarding it mercilessly, his sister Elsa was looking for a way to help the homeland's military effort. She was about to graduate from high school and felt that, as a daughter of the German nation, she cannot just sit idly by while the men are off, fighting.

She went to a few government offices to check her options, and received a few offers. One was a nursing course which, upon completion, would guarantee her a post in one of Berlin's military bases. The second option was to do volunteer work in one of the city's hospitals, and the third was to enroll in an English and Russian language course. At the end of the course, she could get an interesting position in one of the governmental offices.

The only thing Elsa was sure of was that she wasn't interested in four years of university studies. She asked her father for advice, and he suggested the option of hospital assistant. He thought it would be the fastest and most efficient way for Elsa to contribute to the war efforts, while remaining close to him.

However, Elsa finally decided to take the English-Russian language course. When her friends said "English is an international language, but why Russian?" she replied sarcastically, "What language will we use to educate the Russians?"

The course lasted four intensive months. Elsa passed her exams successfully and received her certificate. She applied for a secretarial job at one of the government's rationing and supply offices.

On the day of her interview, Elsa wore a fashionable skirt with red and black squares, the colors of the German flag, and a white sweater. She was tall, with large green eyes, and blond hair flowing down her shoulders. She looked like the ideal Aryan girl, just like those who were in the documentary German films.

At the office, located on 32 Bismarckstrasse, a dozen young women were also waiting for their turn to be interviewed. During her interview, Elsa was asked many questions about her professional training, where she lived and her family's origins. At the end of the interview she and all the others had to fill out forms.

When the supervisor collected the girls' forms, he noticed that Elsa noted her brother was a Luftwaffe pilot. He immediately marked the form with an "Accepted" stamp, and then summoned her to his office.

Elsa stepped in, anxiously.

"Congratulations, Miss Kerner, you got the job!"

Elsa put her hands on her cheeks and a big, happy smile, brightened her face.

"You will be assigned to one of our offices, either in Hamburg or in Frankfurt", the officer said. "You can choose which one. I recommend the office in Hamburg. The work there is more interesting, the office is larger and the options for promotion are much better. Apart from that, there is a possibility you will meet one of our fine navy officers there," he added with a wink.

Elsa bowed her head in embarrassment, not knowing what to say.

"I just want to mention that our Kriegsmarine battle ships are docked there, that's all," the supervisor continued.

Elsa made her decision quickly. She will serve her country in the Frankfurt office.

"If that's your decision, I respect it," the officer shrugged his shoulders and went on: "You have to be there in two days, on the 16th of June. When you arrive, go straight to the local supervisor, Her Knobble."

"For how long will I be there, and what should I bring with me?" asked Elsa.

"This is a six-month trial period. If you are successful, you will be stationed there permanently. If not, then we'll part ways amicably, and you'll go back home," the supervisor explained.

He handed her the stationing documents and wished her luck.

The following day, June 15th, Elsa said goodbye to her father and younger brother. She preferred to arrive one day earlier so that she could get organized and acquainted with her new location.

To his chagrin, Franz saw how his family was unraveling, little by little. He gave his daughter a long hug, and advised her to be cautious at work and with the people around her. He wanted to add something about relations with young men, but then reconsidered and said nothing. While he knew that his daughter didn't like adventures, he was nonetheless concerned, thinking about her in a foreign city with unknown people.

"Learn from your brother Karl," he said eventually. "He is a serious person who has never let me down. He always manages to keep out of trouble."

"Father, you know me," Elsa laughed. "I can look after myself just fine."

"I am left here with only Helmut, what will two men do alone at home, without a woman?" sighed Franz. He suddenly seemed old.

Elsa hugged him again and said nothing. She then went to say goodbye to her friends, Gertrude and Lily. Gertrude, who was like a sister to her, humorously suggested that she fall in love with a tall, handsome navy officer rather than a nerdy, bespectacled clerk.

Her father gave her the address of his old friend from his pharmaceutical studies, who lived in Frankfurt.

"Otto Stiebel still owes me for helping him study for a chemistry test twenty years ago," Franz laughed. "We kept in touch through letters all these years. He is a very nice person and would be able to help you find a place to live."

The train station near the Zoological Garden was packed with soldiers and officers. Elsa did not understand why on a Sunday, when most people were either in church or enjoying their weekend break, the place was so crowded. She suddenly felt a wave of sorrow for leaving her father with only her brother, after her mother's death. It was as if the family was falling apart.

Otto Stiebel and his wife, Anna, welcomed Elsa warmly. Otto was already retired, due to a work accident. He dragged his leg, and his left hand was only partially functional. The couple immediately suggested that Elsa stay with them until she found a proper place.

"Who shall I help if not the daughter of my old university friend?" Otto said with a smile.

The next morning, Elsa arrived at the offices on Kaiserstrasse. The supervisor, Mr. Knobble, read her stationing letter. He asked her a few questions about her education and her skills in German and English. He didn't ask anything about her Russian, a language which she now mastered as well.

While they were chatting, there was a knock on the door. A plump officer walked in without waiting for a response from Knobble.

"Heil Hitler", he said, accompanying these words with the Nazi salute. He then sat down at the table, even though he wasn't invited to do so, and Elsa instinctively felt an aversion towards him, before he even said anything.

Knobble introduced the man as his second in command, Major Krauss, and told him that Elsa was the new secretary.

"Herr Knobble," said Major Krauss, "I brought you the list of the fishing company employees. I checked it myself. Some of the new workers will have to pass another reliability test, they seem suspicious to me. We should ask the municipal police to check on them. If they fail, we will ask the Gestapo to help us. They are experts in these sorts of things."

Mr. Knobble looked at Elsa, who lowered her eyes, not understanding what this was all about.

"Alright," he said, "I will consult Mrs. Martens, who is in charge of the new employees in our county."

Officer Krauss stood up and saluted again. "Heil Hitler," he said, stomped his feet and left the room.

"You see this person," Knobble said quietly, "be careful of him. He examines everyone very thoroughly. Any redundant word in his presence could harm you..."

He then stopped talking, realizing he had said too much to this new secretary.

"You didn't hear anything from me," he told her, and Elsa smiled and raised her index finger to her mouth for confirmation.

Mr. Knobble wished her luck and said she could go home for the day and return the next morning.

Elsa left the building and went straight to the main post office to call her father. She was impressed by the beautiful city, with its bridges over the Main River, the old buildings and wide boulevards.

Franz was very happy to hear from her. Only two days have passed since she left, but for him it seemed like eternity. Elsa gave him the Stiebels' regards and recounted how kind they were to her. Her father told her that her brother, Karl, sent a message that he was somewhere near the border, and that Helmut sends his warmest regards.

The next morning, Elsa went to the office. Mr. Knobble was having a conversation with one of the other employees.

"Good morning, Miss Kerner, I'll be with you in a moment."

Knobble accompanied Elsa to Mrs. Martens' room and asked her to help Elsa familiarize herself with the various jobs around the office.

"*Fräulein* Kerner speaks several languages and is a certified secretary. I hope you will enjoy her assistance."

Ms. Martens was tall, about 55 years old. Her hair was still dark and her face smooth, without a single wrinkle. She seemed like a determined person, and spoke with a decisive tone. On that first day, she already gave Elsa assignments such as filing, answering the phone and other routine secretarial tasks.

During her first days in the city, in the afternoons, Elsa wore out her shoes trying to find a decent place to live for an affordable price. A few days after her arrival, Mr. Stiebel asked how her apartment search was progressing. When she told him how difficult it was, he surprised her by offering one of the rooms at his home for a monthly fee of only 200 marks.

"Our house is large and empty, and we wouldn't mind a little extra income," Otto said.

Elsa was thrilled. "I don't know how to thank you!" she cried. "Nonsense, that's the least I can do for my friend's daughter,"

Otto laughed.

The Stiebels' house was close to her new office. The rooms were large and pleasant. Elsa was thankful for this offer.

Only five days after Elsa began her new job, a great historical drama began unraveling across Europe.

On Sunday morning, June 22nd, Elsa woke up to loud voices coming from the radio in the Stiebels' living room. She was still lying in bed, listening, when the newscaster announced that within thirty minutes, Goebbels, the Minister of Propaganda, will deliver an important message to the German people.

At nine o'clock sharp, Goebbels came on air:

"Dear citizens, in accordance with our Führer's decision, at 4 am our forces, together with our Hungarian, Romanian and Finnish allies, crossed the Soviet border. The Bolsheviks lied to us brazenly and created a provocation at the border. The consequences were dire and we lost some of our men. We couldn't ignore what had happened. Our forces are now advancing on all fronts, inflicting tremendous blows on the

Bolsheviks and also causing them many loses along the 2500- kilometer front, from Finland to Romania.

Elsa and the Stiebels listened carefully, not knowing whether they should be thrilled or sad.

Elsa immediately thought of her brother, Karl. She wondered where he was and what role he played in this operation.

"During the first hours of the invasion, some 500 enemy aircrafts were destroyed by the Luftwaffe on the ground, and two hundred more in aerial battles," Goebbels continued with pathos. "This marks the beginning of the war in the East against the Bolsheviks and their patrons, the Jews. Additional announcements will be delivered soon. We hereby declare an emergency situation throughout Germany and the occupied territories. Long live Germany! Heil Hitler!"

In Frankfurt's churches and public areas, people received Goebbels' announcement with great joy. Elsa went outside and realized that many people flooded the streets to celebrate the beginning of the war. She heard people say things like "finally we will beat those bloody Bolsheviks, and wipe out the disgrace of Versailles. We will beat them like we beat the French last year!"

Elsa turned around and rushed back home. She didn't want to leave the Stiebels alone on that crucial day. As she stepped inside, she found them embracing each other in the living room. Their expression showed neither joy nor anguish. They simply seemed puzzled, wondering what the future had in store.

"What is going on?" asked Elsa.

Otto Stiebel looked at her with a serious expression on his face.

"On this day 129 years ago, on June 22nd, 1812, Napoleon invaded Russia, and on this day one year ago, France signed its letter of surrender in Compiègne, near Paris. I just hope that the results of this war will be different from those Napoleon had."

"It's a mere coincidence," Anna tried to comfort him. Otto nodded, silently.

"I've learned enough history to know that there is no such thing as a mere coincidence. It wouldn't surprise me if the Führer chose this date so he could finish the campaign before the Russian winter begins."

"Why are you so worried?" asked Elsa.

"You are young, and that's a good thing—you haven't experienced a war. I am still scarred by what had happened in the Great War. Hundreds of thousands died in the trenches. Who knows what will happen in the future. I hope the Führer knows what he is doing."

Otto paused for a short moment and then added: "I only wish we will survive this whole thing!"

"I wish the same," replied his wife.

7

In late 1921, Marlene Wilczek left her home to marry Franz. Her parents appeared to have reconciled with the idea of her marrying a non-Jew, but two years later her father died of a heart condition, at only 54 years of age.

A few months after that, Marlene's mother, Vera, fell down, broke all her limbs and was hospitalized in serious condition. Alex, Marlene's brother, visited her every day. After several months in the hospital, Vera wished for her death.

"I have no strength to carry on," she said.

"Lie down quietly and get some rest, mother," Alex said softly, but Vera continued: "Your father left me and went to a better world. Marlene married a German and now I don't even know where she is..."

The next morning, when Alex walked into her room, he found an empty bed. For a moment, he thought that maybe she was taken to the bathroom or for a doctor's check. He then realized that the linens had been changed. The new ones were white and neatly pressed, without any creases.

As he tried repressing the bad thoughts that crawled into his mind, the head nurse approached him. She patted his shoulder, silently. He then understood that his mother was gone.

"When?" He asked.

"This morning, at nine o'clock," replied the nurse, with a sad look in her eyes. "But your mother didn't die of her injuries, she could have overcome them."

"What of, then?" Alex asked, distraught.

"She died of a broken heart and profound sadness," she said.

"How do you know?" Alex continued.

"It was loneliness, accompanied by an utter absence of hope that killed her. Those were her last words before she closed her eyes," the nurse answered quietly. "I am very sorry for your loss," she added and left the room, leaving Alex with his sorrow.

Alex buried his mother in the city's Jewish cemetery, four rows from his father's grave.

Alex was drafted to the German army towards the end of the Great War, and did not serve long before Germany surrendered. Since his sister left home, Alex tried to start a new life; he worked long hours in the same food company that hired him when he first arrived in Germany, and became a valued employee. After his parents' death, he remained all alone in the family residence. In order to dispel his loneliness, he registered for a matriculation course that took place three nights a week. He made new friends there, young Germans who believed he was as pure-raced as they were.

Just like many other Jews who had come to Germany from Eastern Europe, Alex's Jewish identity faded completely over the years, and he eventually converted to Christianity. He fully embraced the German way of life, looking and behaving just like the locals. His only giveaway was a certain difficulty in annunciating some words in the German language.

Therefore, it was no surprise when, in 1927, Alex married Erica, a young German woman whom he had met at the local sports club. Erica, whose mother was a housekeeper for a wealthy German family, had a respectable job as secretary for a trading company that worked with the Scandinavian countries.

During their first two years of marriage, Erica repeatedly tried to conceive, but in vain. The doctors explained that the reason for her infertility was an abdominal surgery she underwent as a young girl.

Erica was afraid that Alex would stop loving her, but her husband was fully committed.

"My love for you has not diminished. Why don't we adopt a child?" he asked.

Erica burst into tears, feeling as if she failed completely, both as a wife and a mother.

Alex hugged her, stroked her hair and tried to comfort her. "I love you, no matter what."

Erica didn't know that Alex was Jewish. He never mentioned it, not even during their most intimate moments. With Hitler's rise to power Alex started to worry, but still kept this information to himself, until one day he witnessed a horrible event.

Walking down Berliner Strasse, in the heart of Frankfurt, Alex saw a group of young SA soldiers, wearing their khaki shirts and swastika armbands, brutally beating three young men. One of the Nazis yelled at them: "*Schweine raus! Ihr seid Juden und ihr gehört nicht hierher*" (Pigs, out! You are Jews and you don't belong here").

Alex saw the hatred in the soldiers' eyes. It was a demonstration of power, signaling that something had changed in Frankfurt.

There was no doubt that the authorities were behind this violent attack in broad day light.

The SA soldiers did not stop beating the three Jewish men until they were lying on the ground, bleeding, with broken

bones. No one came to their help, on the contrary: most of the people around applauded and seemed to enjoy the spectacle. Such "events" were very common in Germany at the time, but they were not reported in the newspapers.

A few days later, Erica brought up again the idea of adopting a child: "Let us do that. It will bring light and happiness to our home."

But since that brutal attack, Alex's thoughts were miles away, and he was worried about his wife. He was silent for a long while, trying not to cry out, and eventually said, in a very quiet voice:

"I can't adopt a child now; I have a problem that I'd like to share with you."

Erica looked at him, bewildered. She had never felt there were any secrets between them. Alex opened his mouth and out came a blend of a confession, an apology and an expression of remorse.

"I am a converted Jew. That's my secret. After my military service, I left my religion, but my parents remained Jewish. They lived and died as Jews. We arrived in Germany in the early 1900s as refugees from Poland. Over the years, we have assimilated almost completely. My parents loved and adored Germany, as I still do."

Erica looked at her husband squirm as he recounted his tale. "Becoming a Christian was a natural reaction to the situation of the Jews in Poland. I did it after my father's death, but I didn't say a word about it to my mother. She was already in the hospital and I didn't want to upset her more," Alex explained.

After this powerful monologue, Alex took in a few deep breathes and felt that a burden was lifted off his shoulders. They sat in silence for a while, facing each other. He then told her about the incident he had witnessed a few days earlier, when the Nazis almost beat the Jews to death.

"This wasn't the situation just a few years ago," Alex said. "I'll tell you more than that; deep down inside, I have remained Jewish. It hurts me when I hear and see the suffering of my people. However, you belong to this nation, so maybe your feelings are different than mine."

Erica raised her eyes towards Alex, who continued:

"From what I have learned, mixed couples are requested to divorce. Think about it and I will respect any decision you make. I won't stop loving you, regardless of your decision."

Erica replied: "If you still want me, after all the pain and suffering my nation inflicted upon the Jews, then I am yours."

Alex jumped from his seat and gave her a big hug. She yielded for a second and then gently pushed him away and looked into his eyes.

"I must confess, too. I've always felt something was not exactly right, your accent is not completely German."

Alex was about to say something, but she silenced him with a kiss on the lips. "This is going to remain our secret forever," she said.

8

In 1935, the German government announced that all citizens must now be in possession of an employment record book, which would state their personal details, profession and list of past employers. In the absence of such a document, one couldn't get or change jobs. In 1938, the German authorities went one step further on their quest to fully control the people's lives, and made it mandatory for the book to be updated by the authorities every three months.

Erica's supervisors at work didn't worry about her not having issued the record book yet. Her direct supervisor knew her well and even joked with her about the whole situation, as she has already been working there for many years. But then one day, he asked her to take care of the matter without delay.

For Alex, the problem was worse. The food company he worked for won a government tender to supply the German army with products such as rice, sugar, dried fruits and different kinds of wheat. The company would collect the products from the manufacturers, transport them to their warehouses and from there—deliver them to the army.

The military demanded that all the employees of companies supplying food and equipment fill out several forms that would ensure they were under strict supervision. And so, the company's vice president summoned the employees to the conference hall, where he questioned each and every one of them and recorded their personal details in forms prepared in advance.

It was Alex's turn to be questioned.

"Name?" "Wilczek, Alex."

The VP repeated the questions monotonously and Alex answered them one by one: address, how many years he has been living in the city, and his citizenship. Everything went smoothly until the last question, about his place of birth. Alex said that he was born in Warsaw.

When he heard this, the VP lifted his eyes in contemplation, and then asked about Alex's religion.

"Christian, protestant," answered Alex without batting an eyelid.

The VP sighed with relief and wrote down that important detail.

The forms were collected and delivered to the main office. Alex was quite anxious about the possible reaction, but two months had passed and no one raised the issue of his birthplace again. Was it possible the effective Nazi regime didn't notice his deviation from the norm? Then again, in those days, there were thousands of German citizens who were born in foreign countries. He relaxed.

Not for long.

In 1938, Hitler and the Nazi regime gained another victory over the Western democracies, with the annexation of the Sudetenland in Czechoslovakia. The following year, Germany's Jews were ordered to wear the yellow badge on their clothes. Anyone caught without it would be immediately sent to a concentration camp. Since he was baptized, Alex did not wear the badge. His employee record book, which he had with him at all times, indicated that he was a Christian.

In September 1939 Germany invaded Poland, and shortly after already controlled Denmark, Norway, Belgium, the Netherland and France.

On June 22nd, 1940, the Germans orchestrated a great rally in Paris, on the Champs-Élysées. Alex felt very sorry for the humiliated French who had lost their land and future, their entire world.

Looking at Hitler's victorious photos in the newspaper, Alex longingly remembered the time he and Erica traveled to Paris. Two years earlier, they spent a full week visiting all the beautiful places of that great city. "Poor French," he thought, and folded the newspaper.

At Alex's company, the managers were thrilled about the war. The chain of German victories enabled free trade with all the newly- occupied territories, which greatly enhanced the company's activity. Alex was promoted and became the director of external relations. As part of his job, he had to meet the men in charge of food supply to the civilians through the main supply office.

After France's surrender, the situation in Germany was quite peaceful. The economy was good and the only rallies in the state were those of the *Hitlerjugend* and the Nazi movement activists. That was the common way of entertainment in those days.

Whenever Erica and Alex witnessed an anti-Semitic event, she would grab his shoulder and they would cross to the other side of the street. They didn't want to get involved in anything.

In January of 1941, a new government order was published, stating that all companies and factories which supply goods to the state would now be under the authority of the main supply office. All private enterprises were forbidden from that point on. Alex's company had good relations with the authorities, which enabled it to expand even further. The company loyally provided the regime with food, including items that could no longer be found on the civilian markets.

As the military's needs grew, it demanded and received more bread, canned foods and rice, while the civilian food shortage increased tremendously.

In February, Alex had a confrontation with one of the clerks in the main supply office. The latter accused him of caring about the army's needs at the expense of the nation.

"I will press charges against you to Mr. Hansen!" screamed the clerk.

Alex was taken aback. How was it possible that the clerk said something like that, in public, against the army? It was well-known that the army had first priority in everything!

"Hansen is the only one who will end the workers' famine. They work day and night in the factories in town, all for the collective effort!" continued the clerk angrily.

Peter Hansen was the head of the monitoring unit in the Party headquarters, in charge of recruiting personnel for the military effort. He was a powerful man, but Alex was not worried. He knew that the food was going straight to the army, under the minister's order.

One day, Alex was summoned urgently, without an explanation, to the supply office's regional supervisor, Mr. Knobble.

Concerned, Alex arrived at Mr. Knobble's office. The guard found his name on the list, and showed him to the main entrance. Alex entered a large, long corridor, with busy offices on both sides. He walked down the corridor, to the last three doors. He glanced at one which had a sign with the name "Mrs. Martens" on it and as the adjacent door was open, he entered the room and explained to the secretaries sitting there that he was called to see Mr. Knobble.

One of the secretaries then raised her eyes to look at him. As he saw her face, he couldn't continue speaking. He started trembling, shaking his head to make sure he wasn't dreaming. He wasn't! The face he saw was that of his sister's, Marlene, whom he had not seen for 19 years.

The secretary did not understand why he had suddenly gone pale, and thought he might be upset about the meeting with Mr. Knobble. She got up from her seat and showed him into her boss' office.

Mr. Knobble got up to greet him and invited him to sit down. Alex did so, his eyes still following the young secretary who was going back to her office.

"Is everything in order, Mr. Wilczek?" Mr. Knobble asked. Alex wiped his face with a handkerchief he had in his pocket.

"Everything is fine. You sent for me, and here I am," he replied. "Mr. Wilczek," started Mr. Knobble, "I received a complaint

against the company you are representing. As you know, the Wehrmacht agreed to give up part of the provisions supplied to the army for the benefit of the citizens. However, we have recently found out that not all of the supplies are making it to the civilian markets. Do you have any idea why that is?"

"The goods we supply leave our warehouses directly for the registered stores, according to an organized list," said Alex with confidence. "Here are the invoices, which prove that we have been delivering the full quantities daily. I have the impression that some of the goods have been disappearing after delivery."

Silence fell over the room.

Alex continued, "I suggest we start an investigation to find who has been taking the products."

Mr. Knobble paused, thinking about what Alex had just said. "Are you implying that someone is stealing?"

"Sir, you may call it any name you wish, but one thing is clear to me; this is not a crime committed by anyone in our company."

Alex began collecting his documents when suddenly, he stopped and looked straight into Mr. Knobble's eyes.

"Sir, might I tell you a story? It has nothing to do with our previous discussion, though."

"Of course," replied Knobble with a reluctant smile, "but it must be very interesting."

"There were four of us in my family: myself, my parents and my sister, Marlene," Alex recounted. "Almost twenty years ago, my sister met a young man who was pursuing his pharmaceutical studies at the university. They fell in love, and she followed him to Berlin, where they were married. I have not heard a word from her ever since."

Alex paused, took a deep breath and then continued: "Let me ask you, Mr. Knobble: who is the young secretary who escorted me into your office?"

"Why do you ask?" Mr. Knobble wondered.

"Her face bears a striking resemblance to that of my sister. I was in shock when I saw her!" Alex disclosed. "Where does she live? Where is she from? What is her name?"

"We'll find out in a moment," replied Mr. Knobble and called out loud:

"Elsa, can you come in here for a moment?"

Elsa knocked on the door and stepped inside, looking at Alex and Mr. Knobble with surprise.

"Come in, come closer," said Mr. Knobble. "Mr. Wilczek would like to ask you something."

Alex could not take his eyes off her.

"Elsa, does the name Marlene mean anything to you?"

Elsa opened her eyes wide but couldn't say anything but an incomprehensible mumble.

"It is my mother's name," she finally managed.

"Elsa, Marlene is my sister's name. She left Frankfurt twenty years ago. She married a pharmacist, and together they moved to Berlin…"

Mr. Knobble witnessed the drama in his office. For an instance, he felt he was watching a surreal play. *Such things only happen in the theater, incredible!* He thought to himself.

"My father, Franz Kerner, is the pharmacist, so that makes you my uncle!" Elsa blurted out.

Alex got up from his chair and hugged her with tremendous excitement. Elsa buried herself in his arms but suddenly pulled back, her head bowed.

"Elsa, what happened?" Alex asked, worried.

"I'm sorry," she said. "My mother died a year ago, from cancer."

The happiness over finding his niece mingled with the great sorrow of learning about his sister's death. Alex slumped back into the chair.

"What drama," murmured Mr. Knobble. "What drama!"

9

The following Sunday afternoon, Alex and Erica went to visit Elsa at the Stiebel residence. Elsa opened the door and fell into their arms with a big hug. Mutual introductions were made, and life stories were swapped, filling the gaps of many years. All that while, Alex had his sister's beautiful face on his mind.

"All those years, I was hoping my sister was living a happy life with her new family. I didn't get to know your father well, but he gave me the impression of being an honest man," Alex said.

"We were a happy family," Elsa replied. "Everything was wonderful until mother fell ill. She was the pillar of our family, of all of us."

"All of us?" asked Alex. "Do you have any brothers or sisters?"

Elsa nodded. "Karl, my older brother is a pilot now serving on the Eastern Front. Helmut, our younger brother, will graduate high school next year and will most probably join the army."

"And how is your father?" Alex continued.

"Getting older," she sighed.

They all sat quietly for a moment, deep in thought.

"It's a good thing that your grandmother, my mother, is no longer alive. She wouldn't be able to bear the loss of her daughter," Alex broke the silence.

Elsa went to her room and returned with a large photograph of her family, taken a few months before her mother's death.

"Here, look," she handed the photo to her uncle. He looked at it very closely and thought how beautiful his sister was, despite her illness. He turned around and showed it to Erica, who also expressed her admiration for the beautiful family.

"I won't tell my father about our reunion just yet. I'd rather tell him in person." Elsa said. "It may prove to be too much of an excitement for him at this point."

Alex was about to say something when, suddenly, a loud siren tore through the air. They were all startled and surprised: months had passed since the last time sirens were heard in the city.

Elsa turned on the radio, and they managed to pick up a few fragmented sentences:

"...in the twenty minutes since the enemy's airplanes crossed our western border," said the newscaster with a broken voice, "they have been advancing towards our capital...The Luftwaffe aircrafts are facing them and we have already shot down some enemy planes. All citizens must find shelter immediately."

The broadcast was disrupted, replaced by a hissing sound.

Elsa got up and turned the radio off.

Germany had been bombarded from the air before, but it was the first one for Frankfurt. They all sat wrapped in silence, until Mr. Stiebel said: "Don't worry. We've only been in a real state of war for a month. Let's hope that the damages on the home front won't be great."

"Do you remember the previous war? Then, we weren't bombed from the air, and still hundreds of thousands were killed." said Alex.

At that moment, they heard a loud explosion from somewhere near the house. Anna Stiebel let out a scream and began crying. Alex and Otto quickly ran outside and returned fifteen minutes later.

"This was close, maybe 200 meters from here," Alex was panting. "We saw many people running to the spot, and also police forces and firefighters. We heard people talking about casualties."

Suddenly, the sirens broke out again all over the city, but this time they signaled the end of the raid.

Alex tried to relieve the tense situation:

"We only came for a family visit, and the British disturbed us," he laughed. "There are still so many things we haven't discussed."

"Perhaps you would like to come over to our home this coming Wednesday, at 5 o'clock, so we can continue talking?" Erica suggested heartily.

Alex looked at his wife lovingly.

The Stiebels and Elsa gladly accepted the invitation.

Alex and Erica left their hosts and walked to the closest tram stop. Four stops later they would be back home, in the center of the city.

They got on the tram, but after two stations it stopped and did not go any further. The street was in chaos, with many people running around, yelling.

Alex got off to find out what had happened. A few minutes later he returned and said to his wife:

"Let's walk back. The tram can't continue." They got off and tried to make their way through the masses.

"What happened?" Erica asked her husband.

"Some buildings were hit in Kantstrasse, and there are victims. It's better we try to walk back home, if possible," replied Alex.

He took his wife by her hand and led her through the crowded street. After some 150 meters, they saw a long chain of soldiers

and policemen blocking the passage to Berger Strasse, where they lived. The policemen wouldn't let them through.

They stopped by the blockade and looked around. It seemed that the damage was worse than had been reported on the radio. On the right side of the street, a large hole tore through an apartment building. It was a direct hit. Several policemen gathered near the Botanical Garden, and it looked as if the garden itself was damaged as well.

Meanwhile, on the opposite sidewalk, a few dozen citizens erupted into a spontaneous demonstration. Some young party members with swastika armbands joined by *Hitlerjugend* members, chanting out loud "Sieg Heil! Sieg Heil!" and singing the party anthem.

Fortunately, Alex and Erica's house remained intact, but they knew the bombing was only the beginning. *Who knows what the future has in store for us?* Alex wondered in his heart, not expressing his thoughts out loud in order not to worry his wife. The next morning, the newspapers reported only about the air raids over Dusseldorf and Dortmund in their inner pages, without elaborating on the volume of damage and casualties. The bombing of Frankfurt was not even mentioned. This was how the authorities attempted to minimize the impact on the nation's morale, and also prevent the enemy from rejoicing.

The next day, Monday, Alex had a very hectic day at work. For some reason, many products were missing from the markets, so he spent the day investigating the matter. When he came home, he went straight to bed.

Erica realized that her husband was preoccupied, and came to sit by his side.

"Alex, what happened? Is something wrong?" she asked.

"I've been worried about something the entire day," he said quietly. "Does Elsa know that my parents, her grandparents, were Jewish? Should I tell her? If I do, her world might collapse." "Don't tell her anything. She has been living her life as a young German Aryan without any concerns. She is young and her future is bright. If you tell her this, it might traumatize her."

"You're right. She won't hear it from me," said Alex, still brooding.

In October 1941, Alex started to feel a change in the atmosphere at the food supply company where he worked. The personal checkups were becoming more frequent and detailed, and employee access to documents was restricted. Alex required free access to the company's documents in order to complete his tasks, but even he was no longer privy to them.

Three weeks later, he was summoned to Peter Hansen, the loyal party activist who was in charge of all civilian employees who worked for the military effort. Alex thought that either it had to do with the previous complaint, or was perhaps simply a mistake. However, he should have already known that mistakes didn't just happen under the Nazi regime, unless they were intentional.

When he faced Hansen, the latter pretended not to remember him. Alex looked at the table, on which lay a blue file with his name in large print.

"Are you Alex Wilczek?" "Yes, sir."

"Do you work as the external relations director for the German Food Supply Company?"

"Yes."

Hansen thumbed through the file. Alex noticed that it contained only two pages.

"I see that you are a Protestant Christian, but that you used to be a Jew," Hansen mumbled. "And there's no mentioning of a place of birth in your file."

"True," Alex replied, surprised. "I was Jewish once, and my birthplace was Poland."

Hansen lifted his eyes from the file, and Alex decided to say the truth.

"I was born in Warsaw. We immigrated to Germany before the Great War, and I fought in the German ranks. What are all these questions for?"

"You leave the questions to me!" barked Hansen, "You will only answer them!"

Alex nodded.

"When were you baptized? Who was the priest who baptized you?"

"I'm not sure, sometime in the mid-1920s. The priest was Ladislaw Jungermann from the Church of the Dormition," replied Alex.

"You are married to Erica Gutthalf, who is Catholic," Hansen continued his investigation. "Do you have any children?"

Alex nodded his head.

Hansen fiddled with a pair of scissors on his desk, going as far as trimming his nails.

"We don't keep Jews like you among us," Hansen said after a long moment of silence. "They only do harm."

Alex turned pale and was about to answer, but Hansen silenced him with a hand gesture: "True, you have left Moses' religion behind you and are now Christian, one of us, but I don't

like you, you know why? Because in my opinion, you are still a Jew."

Alex turned even whiter, feeling he was about to collapse.

"I am not going to tell you what we are going to do with you," Hansen uttered these words victoriously. "You go back to your office now, and we will inform you as of your fate in a few days."

"What is it that bothers you about me?" Alex asked.

Hansen didn't answer the question and just made a dismissive gesture, showing him out of the office.

"You must be very careful and keep up appearances at work," Erica suggested. "You should also consult your boss, Mr. Bauer, who thinks highly of you."

That night, Alex couldn't sleep. He thought about his wife's idea, of speaking with his boss. What would the outcome be?

He drifted into sleep but then suddenly awoke from a nightmare: he dreamed that he was taken, hand-cuffed, to the police station, where Peter Hansen brutally interrogated him. He woke up rubbing his eyes in disbelief.

In the morning, on his way to the office, Alex suddenly remembered his friend, Marc Löbel, who was a converted Jew like him. They continued meeting in church weeks after their conversion. Löbel was a few years older than Alex, and was known for giving good advice. The difference between them was that Löbel was born in Germany.

Alex arrived at work, punched the attendance clock and went through his mail. He then told the departmental secretary that he had to attend some matters outside the office.

Löbel lived in Molbergstrasse, near the Red Cross station. Alex knocked on the door. His friend answered it and was shocked to see him.

"Alex, is that really you? Where have you been all these years? Karen, come see who's here!"

The two friends hugged warmly and went inside the apartment. Karen, Marc's wife, hugged Alex as well.

"How are you? Where do you live? Tell us everything about yourself!" the two said excitedly.

"I'll tell you everything," Alex replied, "but please let me first apologize for not being in touch for such a long time. The circumstances kept me away, unjustifiably."

"Do you have any family?" asked Karen. Alex nodded.

"I'm married to a very nice woman. Her name is Erica. She is three years younger than I am and a Christian." Alex paused for a second, and then looked at Karen, and said in a whisper:

"Please, I'd like to speak with Marc in private, man-to-man."

"Of course," Karen smiled at him. "I'll make you a cup of tea in the meantime." And she left the two men alone.

"My dear friend Marc, I feel that my future has a few unpleasant surprises in store for me. I came here because I remember you as someone always willing to give a friend some advice."

"I am all ears and will do whatever I can to help you," Marc encouraged him.

"I am in a very uncomfortable position with a high-ranking government clerk." Alex told him. "His name is Peter Hansen, he is a cruel man who is trying to fail me. He knows I am a Polish- born Jew. I am afraid both myself and Erica are in danger."

"Alex, I'm not going to tell you anything you haven't already read in the newspapers," Marc said in a serious voice. "Well-off, politically considered subversive people who are not German, as well as Jews who were born out of the country, are being transported to the Buchenwald concentration camp. No one returns from there. Therefore, my advice to you is simple: get out of here while it is still possible. Flee to Switzerland or Sweden, because in all other European countries you will be gambling on your life".

Marc Löbel's words came down like a hammer on Alex's head. Buchenwald! He had heard of this place, but always in whispers. He murmured: "I've assessed the situation as being difficult, but not this bad."

"I'm afraid the situation is even worse than what we know," replied Marc.

"What will happen to us, to Erica? She sacrificed so much, she sacrificed herself, and the question is what for?" asked Alex.

Marc replied: "The situation is so dangerous, that I might have to do the same and disappear, even though I was born in Germany. The authorities' attitude towards foreigners and towards Jews is getting worse. Our future is at stake. We both have to make up our minds quickly. I just hope it's not too late."

Agitated, Alex left his friend's home. Was it possible that he underestimated the dangers he and Erica were facing? Were the Germans about to go after converted Jews as well? Does he have to hide, and how is he going to tell Erica about all of this?

When he arrived at the corner of his street, he witnessed a terrible scene: Nazi Party activists had broken the window of a textile store, which had the name "Wassermann" written on it.

Alex was furious, but knew he had to keep quiet. He then made the most significant decision of his life: he decided to escape Germany, immediately! He couldn't decide whether to tell Erica. Perhaps he should leave alone, without endangering her? After all, what was he leaving behind? No friends, no family and no property.

As he walked towards his home, he started thinking of a plan. He would escape to Sweden, an officially neutral country, which still supported Germany. He would do so on December 31st, New Year's Eve, while the Germans were busy drinking and dancing. He then decided to try and talk Erica into escaping with him. *A German couple on vacation would not draw a lot of attention*, he told himself.

After making up his mind, he felt a certain relief. The only thing that bothered him was whether he should tell Erica immediately, or wait another two weeks, until the end of December.

In contrast to Alex's feeling of urgency, the morale in Germany was high. On the Eastern Front, the Wehrmacht stopped not far from Moscow due to the Russian winter and the need for additional manpower and supplies. Leningrad and Moscow were already in the range of the German cannons. On December 7th,1941, Japan joined Germany and Italy to form the Axis Powers. On that very day, the Japanese hit the Americans hard with a massive aerial attack on Pearl Harbor. Alex understood that those events would set satisfactory backdrop for the happy, victorious celebrations of the new year, 1942.

10

On December 28th, Alex and Erica arrived by train to Rostock, a port city from which ships sailed to the Baltic Sea. They sat in the station's restaurant and had a warm bowl of vegetable soup. It was freezing cold outside. A northern wind blew fiercely, accompanied by rain and snow.

Erica was under the impression that they were going to celebrate the new year in a different atmosphere, in a surprise location her husband had pre-arranged. After all, he told her to ask for five days off work, just like he did. He told all of their friends, even Elsa, that he was going to surprise his wife with a vacation in Freiburg, at her relatives' home.

While they were eating their soup, Alex told Erica about the meeting he had with his friend, Marc Löbel, and his thoughts on the current situation. For the first time he told his wife, in a whisper, about his plan to escape Germany.

"You must decide whether you will join me," he said.

Erica put her hand on his and said: "I am not going to leave you for a moment."

"You are putting yourself in danger. You could continue your life as a respectable woman whose husband had suddenly disappeared!" Alex suggested.

"I love you," Erica whispered. "I'm willing to bear the consequences of this adventure, under one condition: that we will always be together."

"Erica..." Alex tried to say something, but she put her finger on his lips, and said decisively: "We will both disappear. That's final!"

Not only Did Marc Löbel give Alex sound advice, but he also gave him the address of his old German friend, Siegfried Blumenreich, a high-ranking official at the Rostock City Hall. Blumenreich was a liberal who opposed the Nazi regime. However, he kept his ideas to himself, sharing them only with a few trustworthy friends. He put up a façade of apparent loyalty to the Party, knowing that he will endanger himself and his family if his opinions are discovered.

Blumenreich's wife, Solange, was originally from France. She came to Germany before the Great War and remained there ever since. After the Germans conquered France, she cried bitter tears for the loss of her beloved homeland. Löbel had hoped that Blumenreich would be able to help Alex and Erica flee to Sweden via the Rostock port.

Upon their arrival, the couple went to tour the port, and saw that it was crawling with police forces. On the busy docks, workers were uploading and unloading goods while police squads were patrolling around, supervising the work.

"Why are there so many policemen here?" Erica wondered, as they strolled "peacefully", hand in hand, along the docks.

"It is possible that they are afraid of terrorist actions," Alex answered quietly, smiling at the passers-by. "But by New Year's Eve, their number will decline."

They walked towards Blumenreich's residence, realizing that he was their only chance of survival.

Blumenreich lived in an impressive, two-story house on 24 Bismarckstrasse. Alex and Elsa arrived and rang the bell. A young girl, who looked about seventeen, opened the door.

"Who are you looking for?" She asked.

"Does Mr. Blumenreich live here?" Alex asked. "We are acquaintances from the south, taking our New Year's vacation here in Rostock."

"Please come in, I'll call him," said the girl and opened the door wide.

She led them to the living room and went to call Mr.

Blumenreich. He walked in after a short while.

Alex and Erica stood up to greet him.

"We are Alex and Erica Wilczek", said Alex. "Our close friends, Marc Löbel and his wife Karen, from Frankfurt, asked us to come and convey their best regards."

Mr. Blumenreich didn't even try to hide his great surprise, and started bombarding them with questions. Alex understood that he was testing them. Only after he was finally convinced that the unexpected visitors were indeed Marc Löbel's friends, he greeted them with a big smile.

"Oh, God! I haven't seen him or heard anything from him in at least six years. How is he, how is his health? Is he still suffering from pain in his legs?"

A tall, attractive woman walked into the room.

"Solange," Blumenreich called, "come in and meet Marc Löbel's friends."

Alex and Erica stood up and shook her hand warmly.

"Shall we invite our guests to dinner?" Blumenreich asked his wife. Solange nodded her head enthusiastically.

Alex and Erica gladly accepted the invitation. During dinner, while the Blumenreichs had a lively conversation with Erica, Alex wondered how it was possible that this person, a civil servant, managed to survive under the present regime without arousing suspicion. What was his secret? Was it the right thing

to do, turning to him for help? And was it possible that he had changed his opinions and was just pretending? But there was no way back at that point, so Alex decided to trust his instincts and hope that they won't fail him.

After dessert was served, Blumenreich asked them: "What are your plans for the rest of your vacation? Will you stay here, or continue traveling?"

"Mr. Blumenreich..."

"Please, call me Siegfried, and we will also call you by your given names, Erica and Alex," Siegfried smiled.

Alex started speaking, holding tight to Erica's hand: "We are in great trouble. I am a converted Jew. My wife is Protestant. My parents emigrated from Poland when I was young. I grew up here, was drafted to the army and fought in the Great War for my new homeland. Since I was discharged, I have had a steady job at a company that supplies food to the army. However, not long ago, a high-ranking Party member in Frankfurt explicitly said that I was still a Polish-born Jew, and that he didn't care for the whole idea. Needless to explain what happens after such words are spoken in Germany nowadays."

Siegfried nodded his head in sorrow, and Alex continued: "We must escape to Sweden: only there will we be safe."

Alex stopped talking. The atmosphere became tense. Erica wiped the sweat off her forehead. Solange excused herself and left the room. Eventually, Siegfried broke the silence:

"I am thinking about the safest way, rather than the easiest one, to get you out of Germany. I have to contact one of my friends, a very trustworthy person. Where are you staying tonight?"

Alex and Erica looked at each other with embarrassment.

"If you haven't checked into a hotel yet, then don't!" Siegfried said and stepped out of the room, leaving the Wilczeks there, sitting in silence, not daring to say a word. Only their faces revealed the fear and uncertainty in their hearts.

A few minutes later, their host came back and announced: "You are staying here tonight. We told our granddaughter, the one who opened the door, that you are old friends. She didn't ask any question. I'm going out now to check few things and when I get back, everything will be clearer."

"Siegfried, please. We never intended for you to sacrifice your convenience, and perhaps even your freedom, for us," Alex said humbly.

"Don't worry, everything will be alright," smiled Siegfried. "Now let me show you to your room."

Late that night, Siegfried returned home and immediately went to see Alex and Erica, who were desperately awaiting his return. Siegfried started speaking immediately.

"Dear friends, there is a good chance that your escape will materialize as planned!"

Alex and Erica looked at him with glittering eyes.

"But not from here," Siegfried continued. "Your escape will take place from Stralsund, a small town with a little port, located about fifty kilometers from here, and 150 kilometers from the Swedish coast. The guard there is less strict. That port is a smuggling base from Germany to Sweden, often with the Germans' knowledge and silent agreement."

"What are our chances of getting through?" Alex asked.

"To be completely honest with you, no more than 10%," replied Siegfried.

Erica held Alex's hand tightly against her heart.

"I have some information which might work in your favor, though," Siegfried tried to calm them. "First, the trade relations between Germany and Sweden are very good. They send us minerals, iron and its by-products, light industry and processed wood. We send back ammunition and heavy industry. As a result, it's not in their interest to stop boats sailing to Sweden. Second, I have a very close friend in Stralsund, who would be willing to sacrifice his life for me. A few years ago, I saved his son from a tragedy. My friend's name is Ernst Schweitzer, and he is the captain of a small boat, Donau, which is currently anchored at the port."

Siegfried continued to explain the details of his agreement with Schweitzer. Alex and Erica learned them by heart. They thanked him profusely and parted for the night.

They were so excited that they couldn't fall asleep. After a while, Alex turned to Erica, whose eyes were wide open.

"Are you sure you want to join me? You can still change your mind."

"Forget it!" she answered. "Hold me tight instead of talking nonsense."

Alex did as she said, caressing her face and feeling the warmth of her body. Suddenly, Erica began crying.

"What happened?" he asked.

"It is only the stress," she answered, trying to hold back her tears.

Alex understood. The uncertainty was very difficult for him as well. They started kissing. He got on top of her and slowly penetrated her. They made love passionately, and for a short while, all the stress disappeared.

11

The scenery in the Stralsund port was exactly as Siegfried had described it. Alex, in dark blue overalls, as agreed upon with Ernest Schweitzer, walked into the small bar. After reviewing the people sitting there he walked over to the counter and purchased two bottles of schnapps. He also asked for a glass of beer, which he drank on the spot. When he was done he got up, took the schnapps bottles and left.

The next day, at noon, it was Erica's turn to walk into the same bar and order two schnapps bottles. She was wearing a modest dress.

"What is a beautiful woman like you doing alone in our port?" said a voice next to her. She turned around, and saw two drunk sailors facing her.

"Are you free tonight, *fräulein*?" asked one of them, "We are going to an exciting New Year's ball. Will you join us?"

Erica didn't reply. She smiled gently and waived her ringed hand. Then she grabbed the bottles and quickly left the bar.

She walked slowly along the docks, carrying the schnapps bottles, until she saw the Donau, Ernest Schweitzer's boat. She stopped to look at it closely. It was a small boat, just a lower deck and a raised cabin. The German and the Swedish flags were flying at full mast, as proof of the strong relationship between the two countries, and as an act of courtesy towards the Swedish people. Erica left the port and took the train back to Siegfried Blumenreich's home. That afternoon, December 31st, Siegfried and Solange walked into Alex and Erica's bedroom. Siegfried

held a bouquet of flowers in one hand and a bottle of cherry liquor in the other.

"Let's toast to the success of your journey. As things now seem, it looks like we might follow in your footsteps soon."

"Where to?" Erica asked in a panicked tone.

"To Sweden, of course." Siegfried answered. "Only God knows what is going to happen here. Only He can help us."

"I wish we could join you now," Solange said.

"It will happen," Siegfried said confidently, "It is very difficult to bear what is going in Germany nowadays."

Alex and Erica waited in the room until 6 pm. When it was completely dark, they got dressed and gathered their few items into their small suitcase. They waited for another 30 minutes, during which Alex repeatedly opened and closed the suitcase, and keep looking nervously at his watch.

When the time came, they hugged the Blumenreichs and left the house quickly.

At eight pm they arrived at the port. They carried a basket with the schnapps bottles and their one suitcase. The place was crowded with cheerful people. The atmosphere was very festive, despite the emergency regulations of the war.

The couple went through the gate without being asked anything. Every now and then, Alex raised a bottle over his head, pretending to be celebrating. This was the pre-arranged signal which would enable Ernst Schweitzer to recognize him.

As they continued strolling, a policeman in uniform accompanied by a short, stocky man in civilian clothing, approached them.

"Documents, please!" The policeman ordered.

Alex and Erica handed him their papers. The policeman inspected them and then stepped aside, and the civilian asked: "Are you Alex and Erica Wilczek?"

They nodded, and the civilian smiled at them.

"Excuse me for being so cautious," he said. "I am Ernst Schweitzer. I recognized you by the signal we agreed upon, but I wanted to be completely sure that you were indeed the people I was expecting." Alex and Erica released a sigh of relief.

"Come on, let's get on board!" he pointed to his ship. "Our party will begin in about 30 minutes."

To their surprise, the policeman let them leave with Ernst. "He gets good money for his service," Ernst laughed, as they stepped on board.

"Apart from you, I have another woman and two men. You will have a good time over the next couple of hours. There will be dancing and alcohol. Our crew, four sailors and the captain, will join our party. You are requested to pretend that you are really celebrating the new year."

Alex and Erica nodded in agreement.

"If we don't encounter any surprises, we will be on the opposite shore by eleven o'clock," Ernst explained. They realized that the "opposite shore" was Sweden.

The three entered the little hall that served as a living room. Joyful music came from an old phonograph, which had seen better days. A man approached Erica and invited her to dance, and she agreed. Meanwhile, one of the sailors poured a drink for everyone. Alex looked around and felt he was in a dream. The atmosphere was a strange one: five people, two women and three men, were dancing and drinking as if they didn't have care in the world, while they all shared one single goal: running for their lives.

Alex went to the deck for some fresh air and thought to himself that after all, there was a little happiness on board.

Outside was total darkness. A northern wind blew and it started raining and hailing. *This is the perfect time to escape and the worst time for naval patrols*, Alex thought to himself.

No one would suspect a small boat going out to sail on New Year's Eve.

He stayed on deck, looking at the bow of the ship cutting through the waves, as it sailed away from the German port.

Suddenly, he heard curses from inside, and saw a large German patrol boat approaching, signaling at them to stop.

"Who are you?" A determined voice came from the big German loudspeaker.

Schweitzer responded quickly: "We are the German boat 'Donau' and the code is 'Blitz'. Our base port is Stralsund and we are currently shipping goods and equipment to Sweden."

"How many crew members are on board?" asked the voice behind the bright spotlight.

"Five, including the captain, and they are all Germans. We are in the middle of our New Year's party. Would you like to join us and have a toast together?"

A German who invites another German for a toast, especially on this occasion, couldn't be hostile. Schweitzer knew that.

"We can't join you," answered the voice from the patrol ship. "But enjoy yourselves and have a happy new year. Be careful—it was announced on the radio that in about twenty minutes, a great storm is expected to start."

"*Danke schön, und ein gutes Jahr*!" (thank you and have a good year), Schweitzer returned the greeting.

In the boat's small living room there was a sigh of relief.

Half an hour later, they could see the lights of Trelleborg on the horizon. They slowly sailed towards the port while Schweitzer turned on all the lights. Just before disembarking, Alex and Erica heard the other passengers' stories. Two were socialist activists who were sent to the Sachsenhausen concentration camp, along with hundreds of other communist and socialist activists. Miraculously, they managed to escape, hiding in sewers for many months.

There was no security at the Swedish port. Schweitzer maneuvered between the anchoring boats until he found a proper place to dock, next to a Turkish boat. The Donau passengers disembarked with great excitement, not knowing how to thank their savior, Schweitzer, for being so dedicated and courageous.

"Please give our deepest thanks to Siegfried Blumenreich," Alex told him. "We will never forget what he had done for us. And you—without your help, we would never have been able to even dream about leaving Germany."

Schweitzer smiled at them and warmly shook their hands. "Including you, we have managed to rescue 20 people, and get them out of Germany. Hopefully, our next meeting will take place in another world, free of danger for honest people."

They all stood on the deck, and raised their glasses to toast their arrival to safety.

12

Right before the new year, Elsa requested three days off her job so that she could go back home to visit her family. It had been six months since she left, and the ongoing war made it impossible to contact her father.

Two days before she was scheduled to leave, she received a letter from her uncle, Alex, telling her that he and Erica were leaving for Freiburg for the holidays to see some of Erica's relatives. He added that they would get together upon their return.

Elsa was surprised that Alex didn't telephone or come to visit her to say goodbye. She promised herself to tell her father, as soon as she sees him, all about her exciting reunion with her uncle and its surprising ending.

On December 31st, Elsa arrived in Berlin by train. The station was very crowded, with thousands of people waiting by the platforms. Elsa got off the train, carrying her small suitcase, and began looking for her family. Suddenly she saw her father waving from the other end of the platform, and ran straight into his arms. She immediately noticed that his face had gotten quite a bit older.

Franz Kerner embraced his daughter tightly. As he held her, a loud siren sounded through the station. All the passers-by, including Elsa and Franz, froze for a moment. A moment later, the policemen ordered everyone to rush to the shelter.

"The English want to end 1941 with a few more victories," Franz told Elsa.

When the raid ended they realized it was actually a Russian attack—one of its few attacks against German cities. 40 people were killed and over 100 were wounded that night in the attack. The next day, the German newspapers referred to the Russians as predators and demanded a swift and painful revenge, disregarding the great losses the Russians had suffered during Germany's invasion.

When Franz and Elsa finally arrived home, they found Helmut pacing nervously, worried about his father and sister. They calmed him down and started to prepare dinner. Only after that, did they sit down together to hear about Elsa's adventures in Frankfurt.

Elsa told them about the Stiebels' welcome and hospitality, how they made her feel at home and offered her a room.

"This is a true friend, I wasn't wrong about him," Franz noted with satisfaction.

"Do you have a boyfriend? Did you make friends in Frankfurt?" Helmut wanted to know.

"Most of the young people were drafted, so I didn't get the chance to make many friends, except for some at work," Elsa replied as she glanced at the living room and hallway. She looked at the walls and the furniture, and couldn't understand why this space, where she was born and raised, seemed so cold and estranged—as if it were missing something.

Franz noticed, and asked his daughter if something was wrong. She said quietly: "Everything seems so empty without mother." She looked again at her brother and father.

Franz felt a lump in his throat and swallowed hard, trying not to show just how much he missed his late wife.

"Father, there is something I want to tell you, but I don't know how you will take it," Elsa said.

Helmut felt uncomfortable and was about to leave the room, but Elsa said: "Please, no, stay here with us. Sit down and listen to something exciting and interesting."

"My curiosity is growing, I can't take it anymore!" said Franz with a smile. "Come on, tell us."

"A few months ago, in Frankfurt, I met by chance a relative of yours."

"Of mine? I have no relatives in Frankfurt," said Franz. "Does the name Alex Wilczek ring a bell?"

Franz looked at her, stunned. Silence fell over the room. After a short while he asked his daughter: "You mean to tell me that you met Alex, your mother's brother?"

Elsa nodded.

"Oh, my goodness!" Franz shouted, looking utterly shocked. "Who is mother's brother? Your brother in-law?" Helmut

exclaimed.

"Exactly," Franz approved. "Alex was two years older than your mother, and after we left Frankfurt they lost touch, just like with the rest of the family. That's why you never got the chance to meet him."

Helmut was just as shocked as his father, who pleaded with Elsa to tell them more about Alex and how he was doing.

Elsa told them how they had met at her office, and how she invited him and Erica, his wife, to the Stiebels. She also told them about the letter Alex had sent her regarding the trip to Freiburg for the holidays.

"I found that quite strange, because only two weeks earlier, Alex had told me they were going to spend the holidays in

Frankfurt. Perhaps they received an urgent call from Erica's family."

Frantz didn't respond right away. His thoughts drifted to the meeting of his brother-in-law and his daughter, and to Alex's sudden disappearance. *Did Alex tell Elsa that he is Jewish? Did she realize that her mother was Jewish too?* What are the consequences for our family reunion? He wondered to himself.

Helmut and Elsa looked at their father and said nothing. They respected his need for silence. Then he suddenly lifted his tired eyes at them and said:

"My dear children, I have something very important to tell you, something that will shock you and might have a great impact on your future. You may find yourselves in an impossible situation."

His children looked at him, puzzled. They had no idea what he was about to tell them, and how they would react.

"There is one thing I would like to ask of you," Franz said quietly. "What you will now hear from me must be kept deep in your hearts. You mustn't say anything to anyone, not even to your best friends. Otherwise, this might harm you and even put your lives in danger."

Elsa and Helmut were startled, but out of respect for their father, simply nodded in agreement.

Franz took a handkerchief out of his pocket and wiped the sweat from his forehead.

"After your mother's death I went through hell because of this secret. Your entire lives, I kept it in order to protect you. You were too little to understand, but here it is now. Your mother, the love of my life, was Jewish."

Franz paused for a moment, letting his words sink in, and then continued:

"You are the offspring of a Jewish mother. Her parents, if they are still alive, and her brother, Alex, are Jewish. They immigrated to Germany from Poland in the beginning of the 20th Century."

"What a tragedy!" Helmut cried out loudly.

"You can think of this as a tragedy, or as a great love story. We were young and in love and decided to get married. Back then, in the early 1920s, it wasn't a crime," Franz replied in a sad tone.

"Falling in love is never a crime," Elsa said quietly.

"At that time, it wasn't forbidden to marry a Jew," Franz emphasized. "But since then, the political situation had changed tremendously, and what was once a love affair is considered a crime against the nation nowadays."

"Father, think of the position I've found myself in now!" Helmut said. "Only yesterday, in the youth movement, we attended a lecture by a Professor from Berlin University. The subject was: 'National-socialism and the Jewish problem'. His conclusion, which we all agreed with, was that—due to the bad characteristics of that race, it has no place among the European nations, and must be annihilated."

"My son," Franz said softly, "there is no such thing as 'a bad race of people', there are only bad people. There is no 'collective evil', but only an individual one. During the Great War, a Jewish soldier saved the lives of people in my squad, myself included!"

Helmut was surprised. He had never heard this story before.

Franz looked at him and nodded.

"There aren't only bad Jews, or only good Jews. This is true for all nations. I understand that it is very difficult for you to change your mind now, after a certain way of thinking has been ingrained in you your entire life; but if you want to be loyal to your parents as well as to the German tradition, think ten times before you take a stand against the Jews."

Elsa was listening to them and wondered how this situation would be accepted at her office, where she was considered fully German.

The next morning, after the New Year's celebrations, she packed her belongings and was ready to head back to Frankfurt. Before she left, there was a knock on the door. It was the mailman, holding a telegram. Franz opened it with shaking hands. He read a few lines, and turned pale. He dropped onto the chair and asked Elsa for a glass of water.

"Karl's plane was intercepted on the Russian Front, above Moscow. The Luftwaffe declared him missing."

Tears rolled down his cheeks. He couldn't continue. Helmut pulled the telegram from his hands and read quickly.

"Those bastards," he murmured. "They didn't even bother to write if anything is being done to locate and rescue him!"

Elsa burst into tears. "Karl, my big brother, the handsome young man who was so proud of his uniform and officer ranks ...what will we do now?"

Neither her father nor brother answered. They didn't know what to say.

A week later, Radio Berlin announced that in aerial strikes on the Kharkov Front, several German airplanes were shot down. Some of the pilots managed to parachute and reach the ground safely. Franz heard this news and hoped his son was among the survivors, and was being held prisoner of war.

God, please make him a prisoner, and let him still be alive, he prayed.

FALL OF THE HEROES

13

Karl regained consciousness and felt his body. He realized that he couldn't move his left arm and that his shoulder hurt very much. He tried to get up and almost fainted again, so he remained on the ground for a while, on the fluffy bed of snow that undoubtedly saved his life when he fell. He inhaled deeply, filling his lungs with the frozen air. Finally, he managed to use his right hand to get up.

He remembered that an anti-aircraft shell hit the front of his plane. Heinz, his co-pilot, yelled something he couldn't understand. Then came the explosion. The plane spun around and dove to the ground, where it crashed and went up in flames. Karl couldn't remember when he opened his parachute; maybe just before the crash. He wondered what had happened to Heinz, whether he jumped as well and if he was dead or alive. He could feel the freezing cold in his bones. The night was damp and thick. A very weak light reflected from the snow, the light of a winter's moon. Karl came to his senses and began calculating the distance his aircraft had completed until it was shot down. To his assessment, they flew no more than one hundred kilometers towards their destination, and forty kilometers back. If his calculations were correct, then he had to walk in the snow for about sixty kilometers in order to rejoin the German forces.

The color of his flight overalls blended well with the snow, so he wouldn't stand out. He blessed the German Air Force for supplying the pilots with those overalls and looked at his watch. It was 7:20 pm. If he were lucky, he might be able to walk for few hours and get away from the crash site, as the Russians have surely already sent search parties after them.

He remembered that in one of his pockets he had a few vitamin-enriched chocolate bars. That was exactly what he needed before starting his long trek. He found the chocolate, put it in his mouth and started to feel a little better. He began walking, limping and groaning in pain.

Three hours later, he was out of strength and dropped on the soft snow, exhausted. He was afraid he might freeze to death if he fell asleep, so he tried keeping his eyes open.

However, his alertness and energy faded away and he couldn't carry on. Eventually, Karl fell sound asleep and dreamed about his home, about his father, his brother, sister and also about his mother, who was beautiful even on her deathbed.

Karl was awakened by voices in a foreign language. As he tried to identify what it was, he felt someone strap him to a stretcher. He opened his eyes and realized he was being carried on the shoulders by Russian soldiers, across the snowy ground.

Karl's body shook from side to side as the men kept walking. *My situation isn't good at all, even quite serious*, he thought to himself. *A German pilot in Russian hands is a great treasure, and a live soldier is obviously worth more than a dead one.* He learned from another pilot, who managed to escape Russian captivity, about the Bolsheviks' brutal torturing methods. Everyone who heard his stories prayed to not be caught alive by them.

To Karl's surprise, he was thrown into a car and driven to an improvised clinic nearby. The soldiers put him on the clinic's floor, exchanged a few words with a man in a white coat, either a paramedic or a doctor, and left.

He remained on the floor for six hours, until dawn. At some point he fell asleep and when he woke up, he was shivering all over and in great pain. For an instance, he forgot where he was, and then remembered: he was on the Kharkov front. His mission was to attack Red Army convoys in an attempt to reconquer the city.

As he was processing what had happened, a commissar entered the clinic together with a man wearing a white gown and a badge with the name "Dr. Tyomkin" both in Russian and English. The doctor asked him, in fluent German, for his name, rank, parents' name, father's occupation, details about siblings, and so on. He translated the answers to the commissar, who wrote

down the details in his little pad. Karl was asked where he lived. "Berlin," he replied.

The doctor sighed. "Berlin, you say. I studied medicine at the Berlin University between 1936 and 1940. At that time, the relations between our two nations were flourishing."

Then, Doctor Tyomkin signaled the commissar that the interrogation was over. The latter left the room, while the doctor remained with the paramedic and the wounded German pilot. He examined Karl carefully and asked the paramedic to bandage his wounds while he prepared a cast for his injured leg.

The doctor then whispered to Karl:

"This is all I can do for you here. I was ordered to treat you quickly and have you transferred to the home front for a serious interrogation. I will try to delay that as much as I can."

For three days, Karl remained in that pitiful clinic on the Kharkov Front. He could hear the thundering sounds of cannons getting closer to the city. On the third day, he heard voices

speaking in German, and thought he was dreaming. But moments later, German soldiers broke into the clinic and shot the two paramedics who have taken such good care of him.

Another wounded soldier, lying in the bed next to Karl's, was moaning and weeping quietly, but didn't utter a word, just like in the previous three days.

The German soldiers approached Karl's bed, pointing their guns at him when he yelled, in German: "Don't shoot! We are wounded German soldiers!"

"What unit are you from?" asked the German sergeant, as he got even closer.

"I am Captain Karl Kerner, Luftwaffe, squadron 219, wing 15. The Russians took my documents."

Upon hearing Karl's authoritative tone, the sergeant stood at attention and saluted.

"Sergeant Holbein at your service, Captain."

"Take us out of here and back to where we belong now!" Karl ordered and pointed at the other wounded soldier.

"Yes, sir!"

The sergeant carried the two wounded men to the military vehicle, and urged his subordinates to drive as quickly as possible back to the home front.

A few kilometers later, they bumped into a Russian ambush near a small forest, and exchanged fire. They then continued driving north, to the closest town, Rugodokov, which they reached in the evening.

"Sir, look who we brought with us!" said the sergeant to his commander in an excited tone. "Two wounded soldiers from our forces, who we found in Olshani!"

A unit of German soldiers surrounded them. "Quick! bring the cognac!" yelled the sergeant.

Karl felt the alcohol's burn on his lips. It went down to his stomach and made him feel much better. He was then taken to the doctor who set his broken shoulder, changed his bandages and prepared him for transfer to a hospital where he would undergo a surgery. Karl was then informed that his plane was shot down in no man's land, between the Russian and German lines. His co-pilot, Heinz, was not found, but they promised to continue searching for him.

Karl knew they didn't intend on doing so. There was no chance anyone would go back out for his friend on that stormy front.

Karl was transferred to a hospital in Smolensk, however, the Russian Air Force bombarded the city, and so he was transferred again, this time to the large hospital in Minsk. Ambulance drivers were instructed to drive only at night, and during the day were to remain in shelter. Therefore, Karl reached the operating room in Minsk two full weeks after his injury, with his general condition much worse than before. After the surgery, one of the doctors told him that two more days like that and he would have been dead.

Karl gave him a faint smile, and requested to inform his family that he was injured and taken care of. The doctor promised to do so, and asked him to rest until he recovers completely.

At the hospital, Karl began hearing rumors about the Battle of Stalingrad. The stories that came from that front were horrifying. Germany was completely defeated. Hundreds of thousands of soldiers were killed or injured, and tens of thousands of German, Romanian and Hungarian soldiers were

taken prisoners of war. He felt even worse when he learned just how the soldiers had died; some froze to death, some due to the lack of essential supplies, and others from thirst. They had to defrost ice and snow full of motor oil and drink it, as there wasn't even any clean snow around. The high ranks of the 6th Army collapsed completely, leaving their soldiers to their fate of the terrible, infamous Russian winter.

The hospitalized soldiers did not have enough time to digest the horrible news: after a few days they were told they had to leave the wards in order to make room for new soldiers. The next day, thirty wounded German pilots, Karl included, were sent back to Germany.

They wondered why they were sent back to Germany, but soon enough received the answer—as elite fighters, they would get the best treatment so they would go back to the battlefield as quickly as possible. One thing was made clear to the group: they were forbidden to disclose anything they knew about the Battle of Stalingrad or of its outcome.

14

Franz Kerner was home alone on a Friday afternoon, when the mailman stopped by with a telegram. He opened it with trembling hands, thinking that this was the announcement that his son's body was found. It had been five or six weeks since his plane crashed. He began reading and couldn't believe his eyes. He read the words over and over again, and suddenly burst into tears of relief and began sobbing like a baby.

He sat down and read: "I am in Dresden. My left shoulder and arm are in a cast. It's hard for me to stand on my feet, but I'm alive, thanks God. Karl."

Franz kissed the telegram, staining it with his tears.

The next morning, Franz and Helmut left for Dresden. They walked from the train station to the rehabilitation center at the end of Berliner Strasse. It was a nice, quiet building. The only sign that indicated it was a military facility was the guard at the gate. He asked them for their details and the name of the soldier they came to visit.

Franz and Helmut entered a large hall. They saw many soldiers with bandaged heads and plaster casts on their limbs. Some were surrounded by family members, others were reading the newspaper. The room smelled of iodine and ethanol. The Kerners looked around but couldn't find Karl. Then, suddenly, Helmut elbowed his father and pointed at a wounded soldier who was napping on a chair, a newspaper covering his face. They approached, and Karl opened his eyes.

"Karl, is that you?!" cried Franz.

Karl's face lit up, despite his pain. He couldn't believe that his father and brother were there. Franz embraced him.

"I thought I would never see you again," he mumbled, with tears rolling down his cheeks.

With his uninjured arm, Karl pulled Helmut towards him.

"Is it possible that they will let you come home?" asked Helmut.

"Maybe for a short while, until I'm fully recovered."

With difficulty, Karl got up and slowly walked over to the administration office. Fifteen minutes later he returned with a discharge note in his hand. "You won't believe this, they gave me a full month at home! Let me just pack my things, and we'll go home together. Sure enough they need any vacant bed"

On the train heading back home, Helmut tried to ask his brother about his service, and especially about the battlefield. Karl shushed him and said: "Wait until we get home, I'll tell you everything there."

Helmut felt ashamed and turned his eyes to look at the view.

"By the way, where is Elsa? What has she been doing?" Karl asked.

"She has been working for a government office in Frankfurt," Franz answered. "Although she is far from home, she manages quite well."

"Frankfurt? Mother was from Frankfurt, wasn't she?" asked Karl.

His brother and father exchanged glances.

"True," said Franz. "More than that, Elsa accidentally met your uncle Alex there. He is your mother's brother, whom I haven't seen in over twenty years."

Karl was shocked. "So we have an uncle who is part of our immediate family! Is he married? Does he have children? What do you know about him?"

"We will hear everything about him when Elsa gets home," Franz said. "The moment I received your telegram, I informed her that you are alive and recovering in Dresden. She should already be on her way back."

15

It was almost midnight when the Kerners returned to Berlin. Karl hadn't been back in eight months. It felt strange to arrive under dark skies.

"I'm dying to see my city in daylight!" he said.

"I hope you won't be disappointed. It's been through quite a bit since you left," his father answered.

When they reached their front door, Karl paused for a moment. He was excited like a little boy. "There, in the deep snow near Kharkov, I dreamed about this moment." His eyes glittered.

"Let's go inside. I'll heat some water for you, Helmut will help you take off your clothes, and together we will wash you," Franz said with a smile.

"I haven't taken a bath in three days," Karl said.

"We can smell that!" replied Helmut, and they all laughed.

After the bath, Karl went up to his room, got into his old, cozy bed and sighed: "This is what happiness is all about."

In the morning, around the breakfast table, Helmut asked his brother about the Battle of Stalingrad.

"Rumor has it that we lost an entire field army there. How many soldiers were there?" Helmut asked.

Karl almost dropped his coffee cup from his hand.

"Who told you about the Battle of Stalingrad?" he asked his brother. "How do you know about it?"

"Here on the home front, we know exactly what happened," his father interfered.

"But we were told that it was a military secret," Karl said quietly as he lowered his eyes.

"You can be sure nothing will leak out of these four walls," Franz assured him, looking at his younger son. Helmut nodded.

Karl was hesitant. He was sure that the news about that awful battle had never reached Germany. Now, he realized that civilians knew much more than he had thought. *This is not a secret anymore*, he said to himself. The drive to tell the story was stronger than the order to keep it to himself.

"The Battle of Stalingrad was top secret," he started his account, "so what I know is also from rumors. But there are always soldiers who come back from the front and bring the news. One officer, who was in the hospital with me, said the battles were so brutal that it took an entire squad to conquer one house, and an entire brigade to take over one street. There were dozens of similar stories. Our commanders threw division after division into the battlefield, and they were all destroyed."

Helmut's eyes were as wide as saucers.

"How many forces did we have there?" he asked.

"Field Marshal Paulus commanded over about 250,000 German soldiers, plus 200,000 Italian soldiers, 22 Romanian divisions and 13 Hungarian divisions," Karl answered.

Franz whistled.

"Yes," Karl looked at his father, and added: "about 700,000 soldiers all together, and 2,400 aircrafts. But at the end of January, when it was minus 30 or 40 degrees, without ammunition, food or proper clothing—Paulus told the Führer that he could not go on. Our forces surrendered."

"The French army was forced to withdraw 130 years ago, after having to fight in the same harsh weather conditions," said Franz, deep in reflection.

"Yes," said Karl. "It was rumored that the Führer forbade Paulus from turning the forces around, and told him that what happened to Napoleon's army will not happen to ours. Turns out he was right—most of our forces didn't withdraw, because they were either killed or captured," he added sarcastically.

"How many casualties did we have?" Helmut asked.

"They say that more than 200,000 soldiers were killed and 90,000 captured, including 25 generals and about 2000 high ranking officers. Also, don't forget the 100,000 wounded soldiers who weren't treated properly. This is the tragedy of Stalingrad."

Franz and Helmut listened to Karl's descriptions with open mouths. Karl noticed their astonishment. "Please promise me that you will never speak about this with anyone. It could cost us our lives."

"What will happen to you when you go back to the army?" Franz asked his son. "Will they station you on the Eastern front?" "I have no idea, father. It will depend on my medical condition."

Two days later, Karl went for a walk with his father. The city seemed strange to him. The atmosphere was gloomy. Due to the increasing number of air raids by the Allies, most Berliners preferred to shut themselves inside their homes. The happy and vivacious streets Karl remembered were now full of debris and destroyed buildings. The city's famous locations such as Kurfürstendamm, Friedrichstrasse and Unter den Linden were all empty. Most of the shops were closed as well, with signs on their shut doors explaining that the owners had been drafted or confiscated from a Jewish owner.

"We've gotten used to this by now," Franz said. "We only hope that things don't get any worse."

Karl left his father and went to see if any of his friends were around. Unfortunately, most of them were either fighting on the fronts, wounded or dead. He thought of Eva and a wave of longing came over him. He walked to her house, hoping she might be there—even on a short leave. Unfortunately, no one answered his knocks on the door. He tried to find her father's shop, but in all the chaos, his efforts were in vain.

It was a completely different Berlin. His beloved hometown was gone.

Elsa returned on Karl's third day at home, having been granted a 48-hour special leave. She fell into his open arms with a strong and loving hug.

"My big brother, my hero! What joy!" she screamed. "I saw you in my dreams, lying in the Russian snow, with no one coming to your rescue."

"I can't believe it!" said Karl. "That's exactly what happened to me. I was lying in the snow, wounded and crying out for help. Someone, perhaps God heard me and sent me help. That's how I survived."

Franz looked at his three children and beamed with happiness. For a moment, it felt just like old times. But then he remembered that he had a painful subject to discuss with his eldest son: the Jewish origin of his mother. He decided to tell Karl immediately, before his siblings had the chance to do so themselves.

That evening, after dinner, Karl wanted to go and see the opera *Die Fledermaus*, which was being performed in an improvised hall in the center of Berlin. His father and brother tried to explain that the theater halls were empty due to fears of air raids.

"It must be very depressing to see a performance or a film in an empty theater," Helmut said.

Finally, Karl was persuaded to stay home, and Franz realized that the right moment had arrived.

"Karl," Franz said, "we have something important to tell you." "I hope this doesn't have anything to do with your health?"

Karl already seemed concerned.

"No, no," replied Franz, "this is something completely different."

Karl raised his eyes in anticipation. His father was abrupt:

"Your late, beloved mother was Jewish. We fell madly in love when I was at university."

Franz paused for an instance to see his son's reaction, and continued:

"At first, I didn't know she was Jewish, but after a few dates, she was honest enough to tell me the truth."

Karl got up and started pacing around the room.

"What could I have done? Should I have left her? Stopped seeing her? We continued our love affair and got married."

"So mother's family is still there?? You said Elsa met her brother," Karl said.

"I barely knew her family. I saw Alex, her brother, maybe two or three times. I remember he was an intelligent young man."

"Amazing," Karl said. "I didn't even know who my own mother was."

"At the beginning of the 1920s, it wasn't forbidden to marry a Jewish girl." Franz said, trying to justify his actions. "Only a decade after we were married, did it become a crime against the German people?"

"And isn't it strange that, by pure chance, Elsa met our uncle at her workplace?" said Helmut, trying to change the subject.

"I also have something to tell you," Elsa interfered. "After Alex sent me the letter that he was leaving for the New Year, I became suspicious. I went to his house a few times but neither he nor his wife, Erica, were there, so I went to his office to look for him. But the guard at the gate told me that Alex no longer worked there. He wasn't able to give me any additional details.

"I came back to their home a few more times, in vain, until one of the neighbors—a kind, elderly man—asked me what my relationship with Alex was, and I said that he was a friend of my father's. The man told me, in a whisper, that the Wilzceks disappeared in Freiburg around New Year's Eve. They said they were going on holiday but have not returned home since. The police were looking for them, but since no one reported them missing except for Alex's supervisor, they stopped the search."

"Don't even try to find out anything more about them" Franz warned his daughter. "It is possible that they ran away or were killed, and it is also possible that the police are trying to locate their family members. We don't need the police to get to us! Even though they stopped looking for Alex, it doesn't mean that he was removed from their 'to-do' list".

Karl was listening to the exchange, but his thoughts were still on his father's confession. He was flabbergasted. He, Karl Kerner, a German officer and Luftwaffe pilot is actually a descendant of a Jewish woman?!

He turned to his father and asked him, sadly: "Why haven't you told us the truth all those years?"

"When you were little there was no point, you wouldn't have understood," Franz said. "After that, I was afraid it would harm you. You know the fate of those who aren't pure Aryans here in Germany!"

Franz stopped speaking for a moment, and then implored: "I beg you all, please, don't tell anyone what I had just told you. The only ones who know this secret are your aunt and uncle, but they took it with them. Please conceal these details, I beg of you, for your own sake."

A tense silence filled the room. After a while, Karl turned to his brother and sister.

"My advice is that we forget the whole story. Perhaps we should make a vow to each other to guarantee that it doesn't leak. What do you say?"

Helmut and Elsa smiled at their older brother, and Elsa said: "There is no need to make a vow. Our word is golden." Helmut nodded in agreement.

Franz looked at his children in dismay and thought that one day, they will either laugh or cry at all of this.

When her short leave was up, Elsa returned to her job in Frankfurt. In the midst of those chaotic days of war, she forgot all about her Jewish mother, and about Alex and Erica's disappearance.

However, at the local police, someone did not forget about this case. In the missing persons department lay a file with the

Wilzceks' names written on it. Under the names, someone wrote 'Date of disappearance—unknown.' Below, there was another line in different handwriting: 'Possibly in January 1942'.

The file lay in one of the office drawers, collecting dust. Every now and then, one of the investigators would take it out, look through it and write on its tracking sheet: 'No news', and the date of the update.

One day, in July 1943, a man entered the office of Mr. Konrad Knobble's, Elsa's manager. He wore civilian clothing and introduced himself as Herr Stroheim, an officer from the missing persons department at the Frankfurt police. He sat down and asked if anyone in that office had known a person by the name of Alex Wilczek. Knobble answered that he himself did not, but he asked of Mrs. Martens, his acting director, to step into the office with her staff of eight employees.

The eight young women, including Elsa, entered the room. Stroheim took out an old photo of Alex and showed it to them.

When Elsa looked at the photo, a sudden cry came out of her mouth.

"This is Uncle Alex! What happened to him? Why are you looking for him?"

The investigator asked the other ladies to leave the room and then turned to her.

"When was the last time you saw him?"

"A while ago, around Christmas of last year," she responded. "Isn't that the same man who, about a year and a half ago, had

realized you were his niece at this very office?" Knobble interrupted he conversation.

"Yes," Elsa replied, and suddenly remembered her mother's Jewish identity, as well as Alex's. She felt as if a rope was tightening around her throat.

"How are you related to that man?" asked the investigator. "Well, he appeared here in Mr. Knobble's office and explained

that he was a cousin of my mother's, some distant cousin."

Elsa wasn't sure the investigator saw the lie written across her face. He scribbled something in his little pad, and then said: "Fräulein Kerner, you have to be available to the police on this matter. This man had vanished with top state secrets. We will review all the details we have so far and if there is any need, we will summon you for an investigation. You mustn't leave

Frankfurt until you hear from us! Heil Hitler!"

He stomped his feet, saluted, and left the room.

Elsa was stunned. She did not understand how she was connected to all of this. Knobble tried to lighten the mood.

"Don't pay attention to the investigator. He's like all of his friends, they all make a big fuss out of everything. Everything is a state secret, even a shortage of toilet paper."

Elsa was restless. At the end of the day, she took the tram to Alex and Erica's home, where she met their kind neighbor again. Quietly, he told her that the police had already been there a few times.

"They must have discovered that he was a converted Jew." He said, and immediately clammed up.

Elsa looked at him, surprised. Was it possible that this neighbor knew the truth?

"Maybe due to the fact that he was a converted Jew, the search for him slowed down," he added.

Elsa hoped that her aunt and uncle managed to leave the country somehow and save themselves. However, she realized that she might get into trouble herself, as Alex's relative. She went home and wrote her father a detailed letter.

Franz Kerner replied quickly. He decided to be one step ahead of any further investigation regarding his wife's religion, and so he took Helmut with him and they both travelled to Frankfurt, to meet Elsa. They went straight to the police station and asked to see officer Stroheim from the missing person's department. Stroheim wasn't there, and instead they met a man who introduced himself as Herr Hellman, Stroheim's Deputy. Franz handed him a written statement:

"I, the undersigned, Frantz Kerner, born in 1900 in Berlin, where I still live and own a pharmacy on Friedrichstrasse, was married to Marlene Wilczek from Frankfurt, who was of Jewish origin. She and her family immigrated from Poland to Germany before the Great War. At the age of twenty, before we met, she was baptized to Christianity. We have three children, all of them loyal German citizens. The eldest, Karl, is an officer in the Luftwaffe. He was wounded on the Eastern Front and was now redeployed to the West. My daughter, Elsa, who is here with me, is working at a government office in Frankfurt, as part of her national service. My youngest son, Helmut, also here with me, is a member of the *Hitlerjugend* in Berlin. My wife died of cancer in 1941. Since we met in 1921, we were not in touch with any of her family members. In witness whereof, I have hereunto affixed my signature..."

The statement was also signed by Elsa and Helmut. Franz handed it to the officer.

After that was done, Franz asked Elsa to stop her involvement in this case, hoping that he had done the right thing.

Fortunately, there was very little connection between the Frankfurt and Berlin police departments, so the fact that the Kerner children were not pure Aryans did not spread to their hometown. Franz's statement remained in the Frankfurt department, untouched and forgotten.

16

Since the revelation that his mother was Jewish, Helmut couldn't stop thinking of whether he was ever aware of the Jews' suffering in Germany, and of whether he was for or against their physical annihilation. He tried to ignore any answers outside the norm, because his brother was a German Air Force pilot, and all of his friends belonged to the German youth movement, the *Hitlerjugend.*

When he tried, one time, to speak with his father about the Jewish problem, the latter said:

"You must know that your mother was an angel. Her race, nationality or religion had nothing to do with the German tragedy. I loved her very much, because first and foremost she was a kind soul."

18-year-old Helmut was confused by his father's words. After all, at the tender age of 14 he had already joined the youth organization of the German Reich, and swore to dedicate his life to the country, army, labor and Führer! His volunteer work at the organization was so impressive, that in 1943, when he turned 18, he was selected—along with only twenty others—to undergo full military training, and finish it as a Second Lieutenant in the infantry or the anti-aerial defensive force, which was in charge of defending cities throughout the nation.

By April of 1944, Helmut was a highly respected officer in the anti-aerial defensive force, who performed his tasks to everyone's satisfaction. His base was actually a former school in Wannsee, a Berlin suburb, which was nationalized by the military. Helmut served there with five other officers and eighty soldiers.

Helmut liked his commander, Major Kaufmann. He found him to be a serious man but also a compassionate commander. It was from him that Helmut learned that the Anglo-American aircrafts have been bombing Germany day and night, in an attempt to destroy the people's morale.

"They are avenging the Blitzkrieg (quick war) we started against the British in 1940," explained Kaufmann. "The same horrible scenes that we see in our cities today were then seen there in Britain: wounded and dead civilians, refugees fleeing their homes. And this is only going to get worse."

Kaufmann based his gloomy forecast on reports he had seen in the Luftwaffe headquarters in Berlin, which stated that Germany dropped about 20,000 tons of bombs over Britain, Southern Italy and Sicily, while what the Anglo-Americans dropped over Germany and its allies surpassed 200,000 tons. In other words, ten times more.

The officers and the soldiers in the Wannsee battery worked around the clock, day and night, until they collapsed. There was such a great shortage in manpower that they had almost lost the ability to perform the new orders concerning the increasing number of attacks on Berlin, which they constantly received.

On the third week of February 1944, the Anglo-American forces bombed German factories that manufactured fighting jets and bombers. The results were so dire, that Hermann Göring, the Reichsmarschall and Luftwaffe commander, gathered the commanders of the 30 anti-aircraft batteries located around Berlin, and reprimanded them for not being able to cope with the massive attacks on the city.

During those chaotic days, Helmut managed to get in touch with his father, but he heard nothing from his brother, Karl. He

didn't know where he was stationed, or even if he was alive. Elsa, he assumed, was still working at her Frankfurt office. As for himself, he thanked God that he was still above ground. One day, during an Allied attack on Wannsee, several bombs landed on the roof of a kindergarten, just two streets away from his battery. Five children were killed and eight more were injured, some seriously.

Helmut needed a close friend to talk to and share his concerns with, and realized that his commander was a good, sympathetic listener. A few weeks later, Helmut told Kaufmann about his home and his family, his brother the pilot and his sister.

Kaufmann asked him about his parents. Helmut debated with himself for a moment if he could reveal his secret. He gave his father an oath, and promised that he would never do so, but was hesitant. *I may be killed in the next hour, or next week. I don't want to go to my grave with this secret*, he thought to himself.

"My father is a pharmacist, and my mother was Jewish, born in Poland. My father is Catholic. They were married at a time when it was allowed," Helmut finally said to his commander.

"You mustn't feel guilty about this," Kaufmann replied. "In the battery near Potsdam, there are two half-Jewish sergeants, and I've heard from their commanders that they are very good soldiers. I can tell you that there are about 50,000 German soldiers in the Wehrmacht, who have Jewish blood running through their veins. The Wehrmacht will not execute them and lose such large group of loyal soldiers."

Helmut was stunned. He contemplated the number. 50,000 half-Jewish soldiers in the Reich's army? That's impossible!

"Anyway," his commander added, "never speak a word about your origin. If anything happens to our battery, or if something goes wrong, you will be accused of sabotage and espionage."

Six hours after their conversation, a state of emergency was declared across Germany. On that day, June 6th, 1944, the Allies landed on the coast of Normandy, in what was later described as the largest operation in military history. The battle to liberate Europe from the Nazi regime had begun.

17

Ironically, the Wehrmacht headquarters hoped that the invasion of Normandy was only an exercise in deception by the Allies, to see how Germany would respond during a possible future invasion. However, by the end of that day, it was clear to everyone—including the Wannsee battery commanders—that the invasion was not a scheme or a maneuver, but the real thing: a full-on attack on the largest Nazi fortress in Europe.

Two days later, in the early hours of the morning, Helmut heard a knock on his door. On the other side was one of his colleagues, who said that his commander, Major Kaufmann, called for him. Helmut wondered why he was summoned at such an early hour. He stepped into his commander's office, saluted and sat across from him. Major Kaufmann's face was troubled.

"There are few things I need to tell you," he said to Helmut, "but this conversation is to remain only between the two of us. No one else should find out."

Helmut nodded in agreement.

"Now that the Allies have invaded Normandy, it's time you know something you are still unaware of. You know the building on Am Grossen Wannsee 56, the street around the corner?"

"I passed there once or twice," Helmut replied.

"Well, until recently that building served as a sanatorium for SS and Gestapo soldiers."

"So what?" Helmut wondered. "The state built many sanatoriums for its soldiers and police forces."

"I heard from rumors, that in that specific house, two years ago, a very important conference took place, with the participation of

SS and Nazi Party representatives. It was there that they devised a plan to annihilate Europe's entire Jewish population."

Helmut looked at him, stunned.

"You are not serious, are you?" he uttered.

"The conference was top secret, so much so that I am still afraid to talk about it," Kaufmann said.

"This is the fate of millions!"

Kaufmann nodded and continued: "The question is whether they have already started executing their plan."

"It must be nothing more than gossip," Helmut added, trying to push away the terrible thoughts that filled his mind.

"I wish," the Major said quietly.

Helmut didn't understand why his commander was so bothered by this, and couldn't grasp the meaning of what he had just heard. He knew very little about the actual lives of the Jews of Europe then and their fate, both in Germany and in the territories that it had occupied, and wasn't able to comprehend the terrible truth of what was happening.

A week later, as Helmut was busy with his daily chores of checking the cannons in the school yard, a soldier came running from the office towards him and said that his commander wanted to see him immediately.

Helmut dropped everything and dashed to Major Kaufmann's office. As he came closer to the door, he heard a familiar voice. Helmut walked in, initially disregarding the other person sitting in the room. But then he glanced at him and saw it was no other than his brother, Karl, in his Air Force uniform and captain shoulder ranks.

For a brief moment, the two brothers just stared at each other. The next, they were already locked in a loving embrace, speechless.

"So, you two know each other"? Major Kaufmann asked, with a wink.

"How did you find me?" Helmut asked his brother.

"We are both serving in the same army, aren't we?" Karl laughed.

"Meet my brother, Karl," Helmut said to his commander, who got up and warmly shook Karl's hand.

"You have a wonderful brother," Kaufmann said. Karl smiled, "We, at home, think the same."

Helmut asked for permission to speak with his brother in private, and his commander discharged him.

When they were alone in the next room, Karl said: "Something is wrong with father, back home." "What is it?" Helmut asked with fear in his eyes.

"I don't know. I spent a day and a half with him. He is not well. He is lonely. He just roams around the house, walking from one room to another, talking to himself. He hardly opens the pharmacy anymore. He claims there is no point to it, since the medication supplies rarely arrive."

"This doesn't make any sense," Helmut said.

"Most of the pharmaceutical factories were destroyed in the bombardments, and whatever production that remains, is channeled to the soldiers on the front lines," Karl explained.

"But this has nothing to do with father's behavior," replied Helmut.

"Wait," Karl continued, "when I asked him how the rest of the family was doing, he told me that he wasn't speaking with Uncle Ditmar again. They had another argument. In three days,

I must report to my transitional unit, here in Berlin. Before that, I intend to speak with our uncle or with our aunt Martha."

"Don't do that," Helmut said. "I will ask for a special leave of absence and go visit father."

Karl thanked him. "That's good, because I have no idea where I will be stationed next. Since my injury, my combat capabilities declined and I am no longer allowed to fly. I suppose I will be posted in the headquarters, as a coordinator between the Air Force and the ground forces, but I have no idea where this is going to be. Rumor has it that we will be sent to the Dijon area, about 100 kilometers from Paris."

Karl paused. He got up from his seat and looked out through the window, to make sure no one was listening to them. He turned back to Helmut and quietly said:

"I want to tell you something, but only under the condition that you keep it to yourself, and never share it with anyone."

Lately, I've heard so many things that I must never repeat, what's one more? Helmut thought to himself.

"I'm all ears," he said.

"The Headquarters ordered the transfer of 500 aircrafts and 1000 aerial crew members from the Eastern Front to the Western one, to bases from the Netherlands all the way to the South of France. Do you understand what this means?"

Helmut seemed puzzled, and Karl continued: "It means that we are withdrawing completely from the Russian Front."

"That's impossible!" cried Helmut.

"The Russians are already threatening Germany's Eastern front directly," Karl revealed. "Finland and the Baltic states have fallen. On the Central Front, the Russians have already reached Warsaw. In the south, Romania and Bulgaria are about to fall into their hands as well."

"Oh my God!" Helmut blurted. "In my position here, I have never received any information about the other fronts."

"Only God can save us at this point," Karl continued. "I joined a group of officers who intend to change the situation. That is all I can say at the moment."

Helmut looked at him, still in complete shock. "You don't mean to say that you are organizing some kind of coup…"

"I can't share anything else with you. But please, you must keep this secret, even the little you know at this point," Karl said firmly.

"Just please be careful and take care of yourself," Helmut said, in a whisper.

Karl asked his brother to remember to visit their father. Then they held each other in a long embrace, as if it were their final farewell.

18

The next few days were horrible. Endless aerial attacks made people's lives impossible. Germany's large cities filled with rubble and debris.

On Thursday of that week, Helmut managed to get out for a few hours to see a doctor, on the pretext of back pain. The doctor noticed old bruising on one of his ribs, gave him some ointment to rub on the spot and let him go. Helmut then went to his father's pharmacy by foot, since he knew that public transportation was hardly working.

On his way, he heard a vehicle honking behind him. He turned his head just as the car came to a screeching halt. It was a military Mercedes. A colonel was sitting next to the driver, enjoying a thick cigar, and a young woman was in the back seat. "How is your father, Helmut?" The Colonel surprised him. "Is he still running the pharmacy? I must pay him a visit and buy

some medicine."

"Sir..." Helmut began to answer, when he realized that the Colonel was none other than his father's brother, his uncle Ditmar. The woman in the back seat was his wife, Martha.

"What happened to you?" Ditmar laughed with delight. "Is this the first time you've ever met an SS colonel?"

"I salute you. We haven't had a colonel in the family yet," Helmut answered.

The driver opened the car door and Helmut climbed into the back seat and greeted Martha.

"Tell me," Ditmar asked him, "is your father still holding on to his liberal opinions about caring for all the poor people in the world, or has he been cured from that?"

"I have no idea," Helmut answered, acknowledging his uncle's harsh tone. "I haven't seen him in a long time. I have been busy defending the skies of Berlin".

"You are doing the right thing," Ditmar said. "Give your father my best regards, and tell him that I have fate in our Führer and believe that he will achieve his goals."

The car stopped near the pharmacy and Helmut got out. He stood there, following the Mercedes with his eyes until it was out of sight, and only then continued towards the pharmacy. That entire area was full of the rubble of once beautiful buildings.

At first glance, it appeared that the pharmacy was closed. But as Helmut got closer, he saw that the door was open, and walked inside. His father was sitting behind the counter. When he saw his son, Franz got up and came to give him a hug. Tears rolled down his cheeks.

"Father, why are you crying? What happened?" asked Helmut.

"We can't go on like this anymore. All of you, the young people, are sacrificing your lives for our damned country..."

"Dad," Helmut said softly, "don't talk like that."

Franz stopped speaking and looked at his son.

"Words like this can lead to serious punishment," Helmut said. "Tell me what is bothering you. After all, just a few days ago, Karl visited you, and now I am here. What are you complaining about? Do you know how many fathers will never get to see their sons again?"

"I cannot handle the constant bombardment. It is unbearable," Franz replied. "I can't cope with the situation. Neighbors have disappeared, and firefighters and soldiers came in their place. I hardly receive any medication any more, and anyway, I have no one to sell it to."

"Father, stop this. We are all alive. The house and the pharmacy still exist. You must be thankful for that," Helmut said firmly.

Franz looked at him, embarrassed.

"All of you left the house, and I remained here all alone," he whispered. "I'm just so lonely!"

"Well, I'll tell you something that might make you happy", Helmut tried to lighten the mood. "Do you know who gave me a lift today in his car? Your brother Ditmar."

Puzzled, Franz looked at his son, who added: "Wearing an SS uniform, with colonel ranks!"

"Ditmar sold his body and soul to the Nazi Regime," Franz said furiously. "He was drafted to the SS because of his connections with its leader. This organization is the watchdog of the Nazi regime, a unit of despicable murderers!"

"I understand that you are no longer in touch with him?" Helmut said.

"Are you out of your mind?!" Franz raised his voice. "I just hope that one day he will pay for his crimes!"

"But he is your brother," Helmut said.

"If our father saw this, he would die all over again, this time from shame!" replied his father.

Following his father's outburst, Helmut realized what stood behind the ranks his uncle wore on his shoulders and his chauffeured Mercedes.

He stayed with his father for a long while, trying to get him to calm down, but in vain.

19

As a young lawyer, Ditmar Kerner enjoyed meteoric success both at the Berlin branch of the Nazi Party, and at the law firm where he worked, Heckle and Schultz. Thanks to his success, he was offered the position of junior partner in 1941.

Ditmar was very pleased. His name would appear on the firm's stationary, and his future would be guaranteed.

Martha, his wife, encouraged him to accept the offer. She realized that, from then on, her husband would be too busy with both the Party and his new position to have more children, but luckily, a year after their marriage she conceived, and gave birth to their daughter, Helga, who was the apple of her eye.

Ditmar's decision to accept the junior partner position proved to be the right one. He became well-known as an excellent jurist. A year later, one of Himmler's deputies, Dr. Frantz Six, offered him a lucrative job as the head of the SS legal department.

It has been a long time since the SS was considered merely a group of criminals and homosexuals collected from the streets. In 1927, Hitler founded the SS on the basis of the SA, and two years later appointed Heinrich Himmler as its head. That transformed the SS into a brutal, efficient, terror organization, first in Germany and then, throughout occupied Europe.

Dr. Six explained to Ditmar the essence of his new job. He was to keep a precise registration of the SS and Party's assets; to manage the German bank accounts, which were mostly confidential; and to release funds for special SS needs, following direct orders from the Führer or his proxies—Göring or Himmler. Obviously, he would be granted extensive power in order to fulfill that important role.

"Is this considered a military or civil job?" Ditmar asked.

"It will be a military job in every respect," replied Dr. Six. "You will be part of the organization and will receive the rank of captain right away."

Ditmar agreed on the spot. He was the happiest man on earth. And so, Ditmar joined the SS, and began attending Berlin's most glamorous salons, together with his wife, proudly wearing his SS uniform with the golden colonel ranks on his shoulders. Over time, he was given additional duties, such as registering confiscated Jewish assets and possessions, and assessing their value. These possessions came from wealthy Jews and included houses, factories, works of art and bank accounts. They were valued in billions of Reichsmarks. Ditmar sent his reports

directly to Heinrich Himmler, the head of the SS himself.

In order to gather all of the information he needed, Ditmar had agents all over Germany who reported where the Jewish possessions were held. He would then send his people to seize them, with a governmental warrant.

For two years, Ditmar fulfilled his job diligently, even providing his superiors with leaked information about things that weren't under his direct supervision. Therefore, he was quite surprised that in mid-1944, he began feeling that his commanders' attitude towards him started to change.

One day, one of Himmler's assistants, Rudolf Fruchter, requested a special report on some foreign currency that Ditmar's department had allegedly seized in the city of

Dortmund. Ditmar was offended by the implicit suspicions that rose from this demand.

"All the financial reports were handed to the headquarters, as usual," Ditmar answered with restraint. "As far as I can remember, the last report didn't include any new seizing of foreign currency."

"Are you trying to play a trick on me?" replied Fruchter, with a narrow, wicked smile. "A reliable source informed me that you seized half a million dollars in cash from a very rich Jewish tycoon, named Jäger, and you didn't report that."

"I suggest we go to Himmler so he can sort this out," said Ditmar, convinced he was in the right.

Fruchter nodded in agreement.

They waited over two hours before they were accepted into Himmler's office. From the start of the conversation, Ditmar felt that Himmler tended to believe Fruchter's allegation. He swore that his reports were correct and reliable, but Himmler did not accept this, and ordered him to return to his office and revise all the reports from the previous quarter, to see whether there was a mistake.

Ditmar wondered if it was possible that one of his subordinates confiscated the Jew's money without reporting it.

"This happens to all of you," Himmler's voice thundered. "You make mistakes and then come and ask for forgiveness. Come back to me in two days with better results. This is the best advice I can give you now!"

Ditmar knew that any disloyalty Himmler felt from his people had only one outcome: death sentence. He hurried home and told his wife what had happened. She listened carefully.

"Speak with Stephan Schiller, Ribbentrop's financial assistant," she suggested, "You two have a good relationship—or had, until recently."

"Ribbentrop can't stand Himmler and has forbidden his people from approaching SS members. This could really hurt me," Ditmar said.

Then he remembered Dr. Emil Puhl, a high-ranking official at Germany's central bank, the *Reichsbank*, who was on good relations with Himmler.

"Remember, we spent an evening or two at the same concerts last year," Ditmar became excited for a moment. "I remember that we spoke a lot about confiscated Jewish assets, and that our point of view was identical on this, as well as on other political matters. I'll go see him today."

Dr. Puhl was glad to hear his friend's voice, when Ditmar called him that afternoon. "Do you have tickets for a good show?" he asked cynically, knowing all too well that all the theaters were closed.

"No, I don't," Ditmar replied seriously, "but I have a big problem and am looking for a savior."

"A savior? How serious is it?"

Ditmar recounted the details of his incident with Fruchter and then with Himmler. He repeatedly swore that he had never received any report about seized foreign currency, which was not passed on to his superiors.

"I know you are an honest man," said Puhl. "I suggest you go back to your staff and look into the matter again. If you can't find anything, get back to me, and we'll see what we can do. We won't let you fall."

That night, Ditmar summoned his subordinates from the Dortmund branch to his office in Berlin. He asked them to bring with them all the relevant material regarding the Jew whose assets had been seized.

When he arrived at his office the next morning at 8:30, all but one of the members of the Dortmund branch were already waiting for him.

"Where is Wolf?" asked Ditmar.

"We haven't seen him since yesterday," replied Vogel, the branch's most senior member. "Even his wife couldn't tell us where he is. The previous night, she said, he didn't sleep at home. We left him your urgent message, but there has been no sign of life from him so far."

The room was very tense. Ditmar's mind was racing frantically. He began scanning through the material the men handed him—copies of reports that were submitted to the SS headquarters two months earlier, all signed by Vogel.

"I don't see here anything about cash money, neither foreign currency nor Reichsmarks!" Ditmar exclaimed.

"We also know nothing of this," Vogel replied.

"Is it possible that this man…" Ditmar started to say something but then paused for a moment, weighed his word before delivering the following accusation. "Is it possible that this man, Wolf, stole the money and disappeared from the area or even from Germany entirely?"

The four other men in the room stood still. They said nothing. They had nothing to add.

"You, Herr Vogel!" Ditmar ordered. "Write me a report signed by all four of you, describing in detail the sequence of events, including your claim that nothing was reported about any money allegedly found at Jäger's place."

The men listened to Ditmar in silence.

"I need answers to the following questions: One, is it possible that Jäger did have money, and if that is the case, what are you basing your information on? Two, do you think Wolf stole the money? How do you suggest I solve this mystery? Please, sit down now and write the report. I want the truth and nothing but the truth. Remember, we are gambling on our lives here. We are all in the same boat. You have two hours to finish the report," Ditmar ordered with determination.

Ditmar couldn't forget that the 48 hours Himmler gave him would come to an end the next day at 6 pm, and was still uncertain the Reichsführer would believe him. Ditmar was disturbed by one major question: had his agents, his subordinates, been disloyal to him and conspired against him? Were they trying to fail him?

His mood turned morose. What else should he do? How could he escape this trap? He was wondering whether he should leave, but where to? South, to Vienna? That would be impossible, the Allies were getting closer there. Maybe he would be able to cross the border anyway and just stay put until liberation? But what would happen if he falls into the Russians' hands? Perhaps, then, he should flee Berlin towards the Rhine River—to Koblenz or to the small town of Offenburg, where he would assimilate within the population as a refugee?

Then, suddenly, Ditmar remembered that he was actually a German colonel in uniform! *This could open many doors for me on my escape route*, he mulled. That thought frightened him, though. He put it aside, knowing that anyway, he had no willpower or courage to escape.

Three hours later, Vogel came up to him with the signed document. The title said "Statement" and then: "We, the undersigned, declare that...." They described their work in the Dortmund branch, the confiscation of Jäger's assets and, of course, Wolf's disappearance, implying that that man, who had only started his job recently, might have found the money and fell into the temptation.

The letter was written and signed in four copies, all handed to Ditmar. He read the document carefully, making notes in the margins, and then turned to Vogel:

"You, Herr Vogel," he lifted his eyes from the papers, "you are guilty for not supervising Wolf's work meticulously; and I am guilty for not supervising the both of you. It is quite possible that we will all pay dearly for this."

The four agents didn't respond. Their eyes were lowered, fixed at the table.

It was lunchtime and Ditmar sent them to eat, ordering them to come back to the office once they were done and wait for him until he got back. He took their statement and went to Dr. Puhl's office. He was delayed due to alarm sirens and only arrived at his destination at four o'clock.

"Emil, you must help me," Ditmar begged. "I am in big trouble. Here is the declaration of my agents, from which one can only learn that another agent—Mr. Wolf, might have taken whatever money might have been on site, and left town. The fact that he had vanished makes him the only potential suspect. What should I do? I know I should have supervised my agents more carefully,

but there was never any problem with them, they were always very loyal."

"I understand that your deadline ends tomorrow night at six o'clock," Puhl said with restraint. "I'll try to speak with Dr. Six or with Himmler himself, and we'll see what can be done. Call me tomorrow at noon."

The next day, Ditmar was unable to get hold of Puhl on the phone until three o'clock in the afternoon. He was very nervous and even yelled at Puhl's secretary. All she could tell him was that the doctor went to see Adolf Hitler on an urgent matter.

Left with no other choice, Ditmar made a serious decision to go and consult his brother, Franz, whom he hadn't seen for months. He wanted to tell his brother everything, not because he thought he could help him, but because he felt the need to share what he has been going through with a close family member. That would also give him the opportunity to ask Franz for forgiveness for how badly he has been treating him.

Ditmar arrived at the pharmacy just as Franz was about to close. As they walked towards the latter's home, Ditmar began weeping quietly. He took a handkerchief out of his pocket and blew his nose. Realizing his brother's distress, Franz put an arm on his shoulder.

"Ditti," he said, "what is it all about?"

Ditmar told him everything, starting at the beginning, and ending with his fear of the consequences.

"Those people aren't willing to listen to the voice of reason," he said to his brother. "They want to get their hands either on that alleged money, or on the thief. They won't listen to any logical explanation."

Franz felt very sorry for Ditmar, but wasn't at all surprised. He knew those people and prayed that God would never forgive them. Still, he tried encouraging his brother.

"I am sure the final word hasn't been said yet. They won't hurt you, you are a loyal member of the Party, and they can't blame you for something you haven't done."

"You don't understand how their minds work," Ditmar replied. "They will accuse me of treason, for not watching over the organization's property. Does that sound familiar?"

"Oh yes," Franz replied. "Tell me, what are you going to do about Martha and your daughter if, God forbid, something happens to you?"

"After the meeting tomorrow with Himmler, I'll go home, and we'll see what happens," Ditmar said.

The brothers parted with a long, tight embrace, as if it were their last meeting.

"May God save you," Franz murmured and added, "Tell Martha that I am here, and if she needs anything, she shouldn't hesitate for a second."

Only at 5:45 pm, fifteen minutes before his meeting with Himmler, did Ditmar get a hold of Emil Puhl on the phone.

"I am afraid I am going to disappoint you," Puhl said. "I spent almost the entire day at the Chancellor's office with Reichsführer Himmler, and had no time to discuss your matter. However, he was very calm and I am sure everything will be alright."

"You betrayed a friend!" yelled Ditmar. "Doesn't the value of friendship exist anymore? Is it only about your own survival? Know that my elimination will be on your conscience."

Ditmar slammed the phone shut. This was the first time he acknowledged that the regime might actually decide to have him killed.

At six o'clock sharp, Ditmar was called into Himmler's office. He found Heinz Fruchter there as well. Ditmar took the declaration out of his pocket and added his own explanations, as Himmler listened. He was silent for a moment and then said:

"Is there anything else you want to add?" "No, Herr Reichsführer," Ditmar answered.

"Alright, wait outside and we'll let you know our decision."

Ditmar was horrified. He realized his fate was going to be determined by Roland Freisler, the State Secretary of the Reich Ministry of Justice. Most of the trials he was involved in ended with death sentences.

Ditmar waited for twenty minutes until he was called back into the room.

He walked in, trembling. To his surprise, he found only Fruchter inside.

"Here is an order signed by the Reichsführer himself." He handed Ditmar the paper and went on: "He orders you to go to our facility near Brandenburg with your four agents. From there, you will be sent straight to Buchenwald. The other four will remain in the facility until there is a final decision about them."

When he heard the word "Buchenwald", Ditmar collapsed right there, in Himmler's office. He tried to get up and as he raised his eyes, he met Fruchter's; they were full of hatred. Ditmar was shocked. He realized those were the eyes of a murderer.

These are Himmler's assistants, he thought. His brother had warned him not to get close to this kind of people.

He got up slowly, straightened his suit and returned to his office to meet his agents. He handed them the administrative order signed by Himmler and ordered them to go to the SS facility in Brandenburg, where they should wait for him. He would be there within two hours, he said.

Ditmar ran all the way home, with only one word on his mind: "Buchenwald"!

20

Ditmar was one of the only SS members who were allowed to see the confidential reports of the Supreme Headquarters, so he knew exactly what Buchenwald was. Since 1937, the concentration camp near the city of Weimar became the new, undesired home of various enemies of the regime, such as communists, socialists, and, of course, well-known, wealthy Jews. Starting in 1940, gypsies captured throughout Europe were also sent there. As of 1941, Polish and Russian POWs, whom the Germans used as cheap labor, joined them.

Ditmar had all of this information racing through his head. He came home and informed his wife of the verdict. Utterly shocked, she began crying hysterically. It was heartbreaking.

"Don't go there, I beg you. No one survives such a place," she pleaded.

"What will I do? Escape? Where to? They will catch me anyway, so why worsen my situation?" replied Ditmar.

They held each other for a long time. Eventually, Ditmar said that he was going to see Helga in her room.

Martha followed him. The seven-year-old girl was playing with her puppy, a gift from her father for her sixth birthday. Ditmar stood at the door and gazed at his beautiful little daughter, whom he might never see again.

"My little girl," he said. "Daddy was drafted to the army and is going to the Russian Front. It is now your duty to look after your mother. Study hard, and excel at school."

He lifted her up and kissed her.

"Daddy, why are you crying?" Helga asked in her innocent voice. "I am not going anywhere."

"*Auf Wiedersehen, meine Liebling*" (So long, my love), said Ditmar.

Martha stood by the door, crying. Ditmar bade her farewell with a broken heart, knowing that they might never see each other again.

He drove his car to the Brandenburg Gate, wearing his uniform and colonel shoulder ranks upside down. He felt as if this attire, of which he was once so proud, was now mocking him. A guard was already waiting for him at the gate. It seemed as if the facility's commanders have already been updated about the top official who was to be transported to Buchenwald.

The officer scanned Ditmar's file and then lifted his eyes to look at him.

"I received an order to keep you here overnight. Tomorrow morning you will be transferred to Buchenwald. First, though, you must remove your insignia, unless you prefer we do that."

The officer didn't wait for his answer and ripped the tags off aggressively. Ditmar was deeply offended, but decided not to react.

The officer looked him in his eye.

"Are you ready, or do you need to know anything else?" "Where are my four agents from Dortmund, who were supposed to be here this afternoon?" replied Ditmar.

"Don't you worry about them! They won't sabotage the organization's work ever again," the officer answered vaguely.

What does that mean? Were they killed? Ditmar wondered to himself. Judging by the officer's tone of voice, it appeared that that was their fate. He held the desk tight and looked at the officer with hatred in his eyes.

"Don't do anything stupid," the officer warned him "You will be punished, former Herr Standartenführer."

Ditmar loosened his grip and let another officer on duty lead him to his cell, at the end of the corridor. The iron door was locked behind him for the night.

Ditmar did not sleep a wink the entire night. His mind wandered to the times when he worked at the prestigious law firm, Heckle and Schultz. Life was so good back then! *Those times will never return*, he thought painfully.

The next morning, at nine o'clock, Ditmar was led into a military vehicle, escorted by two soldiers and their commander, a sergeant. Due to heavy traffic because of the Wehrmacht forces that clogged the roads, in addition to multiple alarms, they arrived at Buchenwald only at six pm.

The Buchenwald commander was waiting for him. "Welcome, Herr Standartenführer! It's not every day that we

have the honor of hosting an SS colonel. We will treat you with all due respect."

Ditmar was transferred to a concentration camp on German Soil after being accused of something he had never actually committed. The fact that he was a loyal citizen of the Nazi Regime, was precisely what led to his demise. On the same day the iron gates of Buchenwald closed behind him, Ditmar stopped believing in the Nazi ideology.

21

The Wilczeks arrived in Sweden in January of 1942, and remained in an internment camp in a town near Stockholm for the next two and a half years. The Swedes probably kept them there, among hundreds of other refugees, because of a previous commitment to the Germans.

The camp was located between the two parts of the city, which made it inaccessible. Surveillance wasn't very tight, so the interred were able to move around freely inside the camp itself. Among the refugees were Germans who had fled their homeland in various ways, like Alex and Erica. There were also French nationals, who were captured by the Germans during the Battles of Narvik in Norway, and managed to escape to Sweden.

And there were some 200 Russians, who fled Finland after it had switched sides and joined the Germans.

The Swedes provided them with shelter, food and cigarettes, and allowed those who could afford it to keep a radio in their barrack which was considered an item of luxury.

Alex and Erica didn't waste their time, and immediately began learning both Swedish and English. Two years after their arrival, they managed quite well in both languages. In their free time, they attended a modern history class and took part in its lively debates. The lecturer was Michael Jones, but everyone called him Mike. He was a 40-year-old British reserve officer who, in his civilian life, worked as a professor of Slavic Studies at the University of Manchester.

Mike was drafted to the British intelligence Service at the beginning of 1940, and was considered one of their top experts in deciphering codes and radio communication, intercepted by the intelligence agents. He mastered several languages, including German and Russian. He parachuted into Norway soon after he was drafted, but unfortunately was captured by the Germans. In a brilliant operation, Mike managed to flee to Sweden along with three other British prisoners, just before the Germans realized how important he was to the British army. When they found out, they demanded his extradition, but the Swedes claimed that according to the Geneva Conventions, he must remain in an internment camp on Swedish soil.

When Alex and Erica arrived at the camp, Mike had been there for almost four years. All of the British attempts to release him had failed. Still, he managed to send messages to his family in England from time to time.

Mike was an introverted person, and no one in the camp knew who he really was. However, Alex liked him, and especially liked the history lectures he gave, mostly those about the USSR. They were so interesting, that even the camp's German-speaking officials came to listen. Alex and Mike would hold lengthy conversations about the war, and the vast knowledge Mike displayed made Alex wonder whether he was an important man before he had been taken prisoner.

Until 1943, Mike was very pessimistic about the results of the war and the fate of the free nations. His lectures were influenced by this assessment and were therefore quite bleak. He was exposed to official German broadcasts and even to those from Hitler's headquarters, and was further demoralized by the newspapers that were smuggled in. But by 1943, Germany was defeated in Stalingrad. Mike was filled with admiration towards

the Russians. In his lectures, he would discuss the heroism of the Red Army.

"You will see that the Battle of Stalingrad was the turning point of this war," he said enthusiastically. "Even Alexander the Great or Napoleon didn't experience such victories." Alex and Erica loved this change of spirit and his newfound optimism. They shared his feelings, even though they were all still interred. One day, a blue car flying the Swiss flag stopped by the camp's gates. A man in civilian clothing got out, carrying a dossier in his

hand. He asked to see the camp's commander.

The man was a British intelligence agent and previous Commando officer. His real name was Marc Stevens, but he was undercover, assuming the identity of Harold Staubmann, the representative of the Red Cross in Sweden. "Staubmann" was on his way to Stockholm from Uppsala when he was taken by Norwegian partisans in a quick, efficient guerilla act. For two days, he was kept prisoner 500 kilometers away, in the north of Sweden. Those partisans took part in the Norwegian resistance and worked together with British intelligence. Once they realized they had actually captured an ally, they released him immediately.

"Staubmann" explained to the commander that the Red Cross can now provide a lot more help than before, with medical supplies and other necessities. He also informed the commander that, within ten days, he would be back with a general physician and a psychiatrist. Then, he asked to visit the barracks. The commander didn't suspect anything, as "Staubmann" presented all the necessary identification and documentation.

Harold Staubmann, or in his real name, Marc Stevens, started his tour of the camp. He moved between the prisoners, asking

them about their general conditions and the food they received. Finally, he reached Mike's barrack, who was stunned to see his old friend. The two men had a long history—first as students at Cambridge University, and then in the MI6. After that, they went their separate ways.

Mike wondered whether Stevens knew he was captured and what he had gone through. He didn't know for sure, but hoped that this was more than a coincidence: that Stevens' presence at the camp, dressed in a Red Cross uniform, was a ploy devised by his nation's best.

Stevens moved from one person to the next, escorted by the Swedish clerk. He asked various questions and wrote down notes in his pad. When he reached Mike, he gave him a long gaze and then shut his eyes, as if signaling Yes, it's me, Stevens, this is our secret. He asked Mike where he came from and how long he had been in the camp. He wrote down the answers, thanked him and went away.

At 4 o'clock in the afternoon, after meeting all 350 interred, Stevens/Staubmann went back to the camp commander, and asked him whether there had been any escape attempts. The commander looked at him compassionately and replied:

"Our guard isn't very strong, but look around you, sir. Where would anyone escape from here? We are surrounded by the Baltic Sea. I've been here two years now, and I can't recall a single escape attempt."

"I would like to mention," Stevens/Staubmann said, changing the subject, "that the prisoners' conditions here seem quite good. I will report this to Geneva."

The radio broadcast on the night between June 5th and 6th, 1944, began as usual, with Beethoven's Fifth Symphony. Those sounds warmed the hearts of freedom lovers around Europe throughout the war. Then, a few encrypted messages, mostly intended for the French Résistance, were read. They included phrases like "the roosters woke up early", "earthquake", or "grandfather went to bed and left the door open".

Then came another funny message: "The guards arrived at the stables, but the horses had already run away." Then, some more music was played. Suddenly, at 4 am, the broadcaster announced:

"Dear Citizens of Europe, the moment of liberation has arrived! Give all your friends and relatives the news that the integrated forces of the Allies—the Americans, British, French and Canadians, are landing on the French coast at this very moment, in order to liberate the European nations from the brutal occupation of the Nazis and the nations assisting them. Our target is Berlin. Please, stay tuned. May God be with you, and with all of us!"

The news spread through the camp at lightning speed. Mike Jones felt like a groom on his wedding day. He had told everyone that the moment of liberation was nearing. Not everyone believed him, mainly because of the Germans' counter- broadcasts, that the Allies attempt to invade the French coast was thwarted by the Wehrmacht, and that fighting was still ongoing, with great losses to the Allies.

Still, the prisoners were excited. They were already imagining their liberation and reunion with their family.

Ten days later, "Staubmann" returned to the camp. As promised, he arrived with two doctors, a general practitioner

and a psychiatrist. They asked the camp commander if one of his clerks could make a list of the medical problems the interred suffered from, and also requested to be allocated two rooms, in order to examine the people.

The commander agreed and pointed them to the northern barracks, where they could get to work.

The general practitioner was a real doctor, but the psychiatrist was not. Both were British Intelligence agents. They had one target: to get their people out of the camp as quickly as possible.

The first nine patients complained about various medical issues: shortness of breath, wounds that weren't healing properly, various aches and pains. The doctor handled each complaint very seriously, providing treatment and prescribing medication.

The tenth patient was Mike Jones. The minute he walked into the room, Staubmann/Stevens and the psychiatrist entered from the opposite door. They all hugged and slapped each other on the back. Stevens then told the doctors to speak loudly about Mike's medical condition, while he whispered in his ear: "Best regards from all of our friends in the service. They all miss you. Now pay attention: ten days from today, it will be a Saturday night. At 1 am, when the guards will already be exhausted from an evening of drinking, you and your three friends, with whom you escaped to Sweden and came here, will get out through the camp's rear gate. There will only be one guard at the post. You will cross the street and enter the small grove opposite it. Then, you will get on the narrow path which starts right there, and will reach the end of the grove after two kilometers. There you can rest for a short while, then find the North-South road, which

leads to the beach. A small truck will wait for you there, and you will get on. The driver knows what he must do. You can trust him implicitly!"

Stevens let Mike digest the news, and then continued:

"You are four people, and there is room for seven passengers in the truck. If you wish, you may choose three more people who will join you. But remember, they have to be loyal and trustworthy. One redundant word, and the whole operation is ruined."

Mike nodded.

Stevens concluded: "You must disclose all the details to the participants only two days prior to the operation. Start getting ready only after you are confident that the secret is safe. Take nothing with you except water. According to my calculations, you should arrive at the coast of Stockholm after two hours, and will continue from there. I am quite hopeful that your getaway will be successful. Sweden isn't actively participating in the war, so the guard on the roads and on the coast is loose. Good luck! If everything goes well, I'll see you in England, and if it doesn't, then…"

The two men then hugged each other again and parted ways. Staubmann/Stevens and the two doctors bade farewell to the camp's commander, expressing their satisfaction from his cooperation with the Red Cross, the staff in the compound and the medical situation of the interred.

The British Intelligence took care of every single detail. Even the prescriptions given to the patients had the persuasive Red Cross logo and its seal.

22

Life in the camp returned to normal. Mike kept thinking about who should join him on the escape, but couldn't make up his mind. At one point, he even thought about not choosing anyone. But a few days later he had a conversation with Alex Wilczek, his history student, and began thinking that he and his wife could actually meet the requirements.

Mike was usually confident about his ability to assess people. He knew that Alex was originally from Poland, and was impressed by his life story. Nevertheless, it took him another two days until he approached him on this matter.

Finally, three days before the escape was set to take place, Mike called Alex over, in the early hours of the morning.

"How old are you?" he asked.

"43," replied Alex, surprised. "Why are you asking?"

"Would you and your wife be willing to go on an adventure, after which you might be free again?"

Alex looked at him and said nothing.

Mike continued: "Let's be more specific. I am talking about an escape plan. I can't tell you the details right now, not until you and your wife say that you are willing to take part in this plan, and then swear on your lives to keep it secret."

Alex froze. Silence filled the room.

Finally, Alex said, "If we agree, what are we supposed to do? I hope this isn't a joke or a trick. Anyway, I must ask my wife, although I am quite sure she will agree to any idea, as crazy as it might be, just to get out of here." He paused for an instance and then continued:

"Give me an hour to talk to Erica, and then we'll meet back here. I'll give you our final decision then."

One hour later, Alex came back with an answer.

"I had a discussion with my wife, or rather a debate. At first, she refused to hear anything about a plan to leave the camp in the middle of the war. She wanted to know what the destination would be. She was about to veto the whole thing, but then I reminded her of the suffering we had endured in Germany, and the fact that she is married to a Jew, who might get caught and deported to a concentration camp at any given moment. I told her that this war could go on for years, and that if the escape is going to be dangerous, I'll reject the whole thing."

"So, what was her final answer"? Mike asked.

"I managed to persuade her. We are with you all the way," Alex smiled.

"I'm glad that's your decision. We still have one spot left. Do you have an idea of someone in the camp who would like to join us, someone who can keep a secret?"

"I know someone who is ready to sacrifice everything in order to get out of here. I am referring to Sergei Finkel, who lives in barrack number three, with the Russians," said Alex. ""He speaks German quite well because he had lived among them. He claims he is originally a Bessarabian Jew, who fought on the Finnish Front against the Finns and the Germans in 1941. He was captured and taken prisoner but escaped and arrived here in 1943. He said that his two years in captivity were spent in a POW camp near Helsinki, where he was tortured by the German guards. He learned from other Bessarabian soldiers that in June of 1941, his family and many other Jews from the region were brutally murdered. Since then, he has been anxious to exact his family's revenge. In my opinion, this man is trustworthy and ready for anything."

"Then here is your first mission," Mike explained. "Go speak with him, find out how far he is willing to go in order to escape. When you have all the details, have him swear to secrecy, and tell him about the little group we are organizing. Don't mention anything about assistance from outside the camp!"

On the first Saturday of October 1944, in the afternoon hours, Mike checked the rear gate, then patrolled the area and at the grove across the road. After he was done, he went to meet his three British friends, Alex, Erica and Sergei, who had decided to join the group. Mike gave them the schedule and described the upcoming events in detail.

Mike was impressed by the Bessarabian man. Sergei told him he was 26 years old, and described the suffering he underwent in the POW camp, how he had been repeatedly tortured by the German and Finnish soldiers. He wept when he described how his family was murdered by the Nazis. The man was a loose cannon, ready to explode at any moment.

It started raining. The clouds would play an important role in camouflaging their escape. At 1 am, the group gathered behind the barrack adjacent to the rear gate.

One of Mike's English friends, Dan Armstrong, who spoke Swedish very well, approached the guard on post with a few bottles of beer, and started a conversation with him. The guard was already a little intoxicated, and after consuming another bottle from Dan's stock, had almost fallen asleep. While Dan was busy keeping the conversation with the guard alive, the group safely left the camp. Dan joined them soon after. No one even

stopped him. He crossed the road quickly and found his friends making their way through the trees.

They found the narrow path that went through the grove, and followed it until they reached the North-South road.

Fifteen minutes later, which felt like an eternity, they heard a car beep, followed by a sharp whistle-blow. They made their way towards the sound. To their right, they identified a small truck and quietly climbed in.

The truck was stuffy and crowded, but they didn't complain—it was their road to freedom. The driver gave them sandwiches and juice and drove them to the nearby coast town of Lysekil. After three hours of bumpy travel, they reached the little town, located on a bay somewhat north of Gothenburg. They got out of the vehicle, stretched their legs and breathed in the fresh sea air. The sky above glittered with a million stars that looked like pearls. It was a wonderful night for a getaway.

As they lay down on the damp sand, Mike noticed someone signaling to them in Morse code. He deciphered it, then told the group to get ready: a boat would come for them in five minutes. The boat got very close and stopped about twenty meters away from the shore. It was a peculiar vessel; its sails were stretched, even though there was no wind. At its center was a

turret, on which there was a swiveling flashlight.

The Captain met them on board, welcomed them and showed them the way down a narrow ladder under the deck. They went down into an elongated room that was furnished with a few sofas and a table two bottles of whiskey and a plate of cookies on it.

"I am Henry Lauren," the Captain said in broken German, a warm smile on his face. "I am English, the son of French

immigrants. I participated in the Battle of Dunkirk in 1940, and managed to survive and return to England. I am now at the service of His Majesty, King George the 6th. You are sailing onboard 'The Rhineland', but this is just her operational nickname. She is actually part of the British Navy."

The Captain explained that now, after the invasion to Normandy, Baltic and the North Seas were almost clear of enemy battleships.

"The Germans are trying to save their asses," Captain Lauren said in his cynical tone. "If they have any active planes or maritime vessels, then they must be hidden in the ports they are still controlling."

The Captain described their route from Lysekil to the open sea. They would wait out in sea for a few hours, then cross the Straits of Skajerk, enter the Northern Sea and head west. Fifty kilometers later, the Captain would steer the boat southward, towards the island of Texel in northern Holland. This island was liberated by the Allies ten days earlier. Texel was 300 kilometers away, and Lauren hoped to make it there in twelve hours, despite the weather which was predicted to be rough: winds, heavy rain and high waves. He told his passengers they should keep a vomiting bag close by.

When he finished explaining everything, the Captain suggested they raise a toast for the success of their operation.

"Long live the King! Long live the British Navy! Long live the Anglo-American Alliance!" said Alex. Everyone applauded happily.

"*Lehayim*!" Alex called out, using the Hebrew toast meaning "to life". He hugged Erica with tears of excitement in his eyes.

And so began the path to liberation of the seven refugees, who managed to escape to freedom in the middle of the war.

Shortly after they began their voyage, the skies were covered with dark clouds and heavy rain began falling. The boat hurled across ominous, three-meter-high waves. They all had to use the vomiting bags.

Erica felt very ill and Alex didn't know how to help. The Captain gave her a pill to stop the vomiting. Noticing the worry on his passengers' faces, he gently said:

"Don't worry, we're sailing on one of the greatest wonders of the British fleet. This is actually the star model of the British Commando. Its engines are strong, and its structure enables to withstand heavy storms."

They continued their journey for about ten hours. It was pitch black outside, and the air was so thick one could have cut it with a knife. Captain Lauren said that if the storm calms down, they would be able to see Texel in two to three hours.

The storm did calm down. On the dawn of Sunday morning, October 8th 1944, the group docked in the island of Texel. Erica and Alex held hands, both on the verge of tears. They took a deep breath; it was an incredible moment of freedom.

Mike went to meet the Island's officer on duty, a British captain with a long mustache, and introduced himself. Upon learning he was speaking with a major in the British Intelligence, the officer stood at attention and saluted. Mike told him about all the years he had spent in the internment camp, as well as the life stories of the other refugees. The Captain rushed to bring them something to eat, and then saw to it that they would receive proper accommodations at one of the port's empty barracks, which was indented for military forces.

The next morning, the refugees were interviewed by Colonel Wilson, the Allies commander on the island. He listened to their stories and took notes.

"I am 43 and was born in Poland as a Jew, but I converted. This is Erica, my wife, a Christian born in Germany," Alex began telling him.

Wilson thought that the couple's story sounded peculiar. He couldn't understand how German citizens managed to escape the horrors of the Nazi regime, and why they decided to risk everything.

Alex then recounted, in detail, how his family escaped from Poland to Germany in the early 1900s, after a lengthy wave of pogroms against the Jews and amid ongoing anti-Semitism; how he was drafted to the German army during the Great War, and how the life of the Jews began taking a terrible turn for the worse starting in 1933.

"In the years since the war against the USSR began, we haven't had one calm night," Alex explained. "I worked in a factory that supplied food to industry workers and to the Wehrmacht. Someone who wanted to harm me told my superiors a false story, that some of the provisions had disappeared. I was about to be arrested, but thanks to a few loyal friends, we managed to escape to Sweden via sea at the very last moment."

Wilson listened carefully and then said, "You are the only German citizens I've met in a while. Tell me more about the atmosphere in Germany nowadays."

"I'm sorry, but I can't. It's been more than two years since we left. I have no idea what it's like there at the moment."

Wilson was disappointed. He was hoping to find out how the Germans had reacted to the aerial bombardments and the Invasion of Normandy.

Alex noticed the Captain's disappointment and added, "I can tell you one thing, though; when we lived in Frankfurt, the Allies' aerial attacks were becoming more and more powerful and frequent, mainly on industrial plants and military targets. The current situation is quite dire. The Allies are bombarding Germany without any interruption or resistance. In my opinion, the war is over. Germany is defeated, but I don't think it has realized the depth of this defeat quite yet."

Wilson did not expect such a deep analysis. Ironically, a German refugee, whom he accidently bumped into, managed to clarify the situation for him.

"But why didn't the German people rise up against their leader's tyranny?!" Wilson wondered.

Alex smirked bitterly.

"This isn't surprising at all," he said. "The most important factor that has been keeping the regime in power since the early '30s is the loyalty of most of the German citizens. If you check the Germans' attitude towards their leaders throughout history, you'll discover that they have never rebelled. There is a profound obedience in their behavior towards those in power. They are as loyal and obedient as a herd to its shepherd, even if the shepherd is a mad, evil person."

The colonel nodded.

"The end is coming, Colonel. We all know it, it's just the Germans who haven't understood their situation yet," Alex concluded.

Wilson shook Alex's hand enthusiastically. "Thank you for this information."

"I feel very bad for my homeland," Alex said, matter-of-fact.

Wilson put his arm around Alex's shoulder. "Don't feel this way. You and your wife could take part in the propaganda efforts of a new Germany, the kind we want after this whole thing is over. You could do a great job!"

Alex looked at him, confused.

"It's quite practical," the colonel said. "I will transfer your names to my supervisors and we will consider how to put your love to pre-war, pre-Nazi Germany to the nation's best use."

Alex, Erica and the rest of the group stayed on the island for two more weeks. They felt as if they were living in a dream. But the Russian inmate, Sergei Finkel, disappeared. Apparently, he was sent on a special mission regarding the Russian POWs who were newly liberated from the factories where they worked in occupied France.

One thing that impressed Alex was the close relationship between the British officers and the regular troops stationed on the island. It was an odd phenomenon for him, because he remembered the strong discipline in the Wehrmacht. If a German officer so much as approached a group of soldiers, they would immediately stop whatever they were doing and salute.

This helped Alex understand the difference between a totalitarian regime and a democratic one. He then started becoming more interested in reading English newspapers, and learned that there were still fierce battles on the Western Front and in the Netherlands, but that France was almost completely liberated after the Allies took over the cities of Toulon and Marseille, followed by the Provence region.

Alex felt that the projection he had given Colonel Wilson a few days earlier was coming true. Germany was defeated, but still refused to accept this fact.

A few days later, Mike and the three other British agents came to the Wilczeks' barracks to say goodbye. They were called back to England on a special assignment. Alex was frustrated.

"What about us?" he asked.

"Be patient, my friend," Mike suggested. "Don't worry! We are still at war, and no one has the time to look for you. I'll talk to the island commander and ask whether he can give you something useful to do."

Mike never got back to him. That night, he and his friends left the island.

23

Winter arrived, and heavy storms ravaged the island. Alex and Erica suffered greatly from the weather. They were left alone in their barrack, and when they looked out of the window they couldn't see anything, even though it was the early afternoon. The rain hit the roof forcefully, and they felt as if it was also hitting their souls.

They were afraid for their future, feeling its uncertainty. They have been doing nothing for months and felt dismay and despair. Most of the soldiers who had been stationed on the island left in the beginning of the month, and they felt quite lonely.

On November 9th, a soldier came running from Wilson's office, asking them to come with him immediately.

"You go without me, you can represent me as well," Erica said. "No." Alex replied "Please join me, I am not going to do anything without you. Together, we will hear what they have to say."

Commander Wilson asked them to sit down and served them some hot tea.

"Madam, Sir, we have an assignment we think might suit you." Alex and Erica's eyes glittered with hope.

"Are you willing to work for the Allies?" the officer asked them, "Or you would perhaps rather wait here until the war is over, and return safely to your homeland?"

The two looked at each other and still said nothing.

"Your answer is very important to us," Wilson continued. "You are young and can contribute a lot to the Allies' efforts. By the way, I received warm recommendations about you from Major Mike Jones. He can vouch for your loyalty to the liberators of Europe."

Alex and Erica were stunned. They hadn't expected that. Alex asked for permission to speak with his wife in private. The commander agreed and left them alone in his office.

"I am a little reluctant," Erica said.

Alex put his hand on her shoulder and looked into her eyes. "Erica," he said softly, "I am not an adventurous person, but let's hear what he has to offer us. Maybe we will be able to help our beloved homeland. The only other option is to rot here until the war is over."

Erica sighed.

"Let's go for it," Alex cried out. "We can do anything they ask us to, can't we?"

"I agreed to leave Germany and run away with you," Erica said quietly, "so I'll stick with you now as well."

Alex bent down and kissed her softly. Her lips were cold, and he hugged her tight. Before he could say anything else, there was a knock on the door, and Colonel Wilson returned.

"We are ready to serve the Allies and will do whatever is requested," Alex said decisively.

"I had hoped this would be your answer," Wilson said in a satisfied tone. "Alright, your mission is a humanitarian one, to help the German people who need a fresh start. You will be sent to Strasbourg accompanied by our unit. We are anticipating the fall of Germany any day now. You will enter the city and help the Red Cross organize the thousands of German refugees who fled their homeland. Talk to them, Germans to Germans, and try to help them with anything they need. At the same time, use the opportunity to retrieve relevant information about the situation in Germany: morale, food, transportation, and if possible—information about movement and deployment of the military forces."

Alex and Erica looked at each other.

"Please, be careful with how you conduct yourselves. After all, you're not Intelligence agents," added Wilson.

Erica sighed and the colonel smiled at her. "Get ready to leave tomorrow morning. You will be briefed upon arrival.

"You will not be alone," he encouraged them. "You are part of a group comprised of several other German citizens, who will be spread across the border. Don't worry, this is not espionage: it is humanitarian assistance with a bit of intelligence gathering, that's all."

Wilson gave them the names of the officers they would need to contact in Strasbourg, as well as a letter they were to present upon arrival. He assured them that their names had already been given to the headquarters in Strasbourg, and gave them 50,000 French francs, a sum that would sustain them for a while. He then shook their hands and wished them luck.

The Wilczeks returned to their room and hugged each other with excitement for a long time. The adventure they were about to embark on was both frightening and stimulating.

"Are we ready, Alex?" asked Erica.

"With you, I am ready for anything. We managed to escape Germany and Sweden, and we can do this now, together."

24

On November 10th, 1944, Alex and Erica left the Island of Texel on board a British guard ship. A storm was raging. On board were some fifty soldiers as well as a group of journalists, reporting on the latest combats over the Dutch islands. They sailed for 320 kilometers of pouring rain and poor visibility.

They turned off all the lights on the boat before entering the Port of Dunkirk. They had to follow blackout regulations, in case the Germans would return to bombard the city. The journalists told them that the Germans fought frantically. They suffered many losses, but so did the British.

The ship's Captain advised Alex and Erica to remain on board overnight, and was kind enough to offer them his personal cabin. Erica agreed and went to lie down and gather some strength for the difficult days ahead, while Alex remained on deck with the journalists.

The French managed to restore their public transportation system quickly. The next morning, the Wilczeks took a train to Lille, 70 kilometers away. They arrived at night and took another train, to Metz, some 270 kilometers away. Erica complained that she was tired and that her legs hurt, and Alex was attentive and decided they should stay for the night. Metz, the city once known for its beauty, was in ruins, sad and lifeless.

Over the next few days, they saw similar scenes throughout liberated France; towns and villages were reduced to rubble. As the Germans withdrew, they unleashed their fury not only on the people but also on the buildings and public institutions. What

Alex and Erica witnessed was the result of four years of suffering and despair. At least now, the French could start smiling again.

In the beginning of December 1944, the couple arrived in Strasbourg. A few days prior to their arrival, the city was liberated by the acclaimed General Leclerc, who headed the French 2nd Armored Division. The beautiful city had become the administrative center for the Ally forces still fighting in the region.

Alex and Erica, wearing the khaki uniforms they received from the British, arrived in the intelligence office set up by the Allies, and asked to see Colonel Fred Lord. They were told that he was out of town; meanwhile, they would be given a room and meals.

Over the next days, they toured the city, admiring its beauty and visiting historical sites such as the old university and the cathedral. A few of the city's sites and institutions were damaged, but most were almost intact.

When Colonel Lord returned to his office, he saw Alex and Erica immediately. They gave him Colonel Wilson's letter and told him their story. Colonel Lord was overwhelmed by their long escape route, starting in 1942 Germany, and asked them to sit and wait patiently. He guaranteed that once the fighting moved further away, they would be able to start their mission. He gave them 100,000 French francs as an advance, as well as permanent accommodations, then had their picture taken for an official document, confirming that they were on His Majesty's service.

The couple was highly impressed with the Colonel. He had a charismatic personality and was well-versed in all the small details, which officers at his rank tended to leave to their juniors.

The days passed, and Alex and Erica were still waiting. They went back to check with Colonel Lord, but his secretary explained that the battles in the south of Belgium had begun, and that the Colonel and his forces were sent there.

The Wilczeks waited for another three weeks, doing nothing. On January 10th,1945, they returned to Colonel Lord's office. As they arrived, they were surprised to see a joyful atmosphere and a lot of commotion. Thanks to their official documents, they were allowed to enter a large hall, where Colonel Lord was holding a press conference about the Battle of the Ardennes. He explained that the battle had begun as a result of the American's indifference; they were certain that the Germans were so severely beaten, that they wouldn't be able to start another offensive. The German targets were the cities of Antwerp, Liege and perhaps also Reims, in France. The Ally Forces were called in to fight. They suffered great losses: more than 10,000 dead, some 45,000 wounded and over 20,000 missing or captured. Over 120,000 German soldiers were killed, wounded or captured.

At the end of the press conference, the Colonel met the Wilczeks and apologized for their long wait. He assured them that they would soon meet a refugee, who had just fled Germany and was due to arrive in Strasbourg shortly.

The Colonel said that this man would provide them with the most up-to-date information he had about Germany's condition, but didn't elaborate any further.

"You will know everything when you meet him," he said mysteriously.

On January 20th, Alex and Erica were summoned to the Colonel's office to meet the German refugee. He seemed about 25 years old and was dressed in the British khaki uniform, with

no insignia or ranks. Three more men, whom they had not met before, were also in the room: a couple named Julius and Berta Müller, and an American officer—an older man the

Colonel referred to as Major Tom. Colonel Lord invited the Wilczeks to join them around the table.

The young man had nice features, and Alex thought his face seemed familiar, but then remembered the many faces he had seen since leaving his home.

"Ladies and gentlemen," the Colonel began the meeting, "I am honored to introduce you to Major Karl Kerner, a former German Air Force pilot, who was captured by our forces and is now willing to join us in helping to liberate his country."

When he heard the name, Alex began trembling. He raised his hand as if asking for permission to speak, but then lowered it quickly, before anyone noticed.

"I would like to remind you that you are here of your own free will, and swore allegiance to the Allied forces," the Colonel went on. "We need German speakers, who will be able to locate other defectors, whether civilians or soldiers. The relevant information you gather from those people will help bring this war to its swift end, and hasten the restoration of Germany. This is our main task."

The Colonel looked at all of them and then added: "I want you to meet someone else", he pointed at the Major. "This is Major Tom, an American soldier and war hero, who fought in North Africa and participated in the Invasion of Normandy. He speaks German, and will supervise and monitor your work and then report back to me."

Then the Colonel turned back to Karl: "Major Kerner was captured near the Moselle with the 32nd Infantry Brigade, and immediately expressed his willingness to cooperate with us, knowing that Germany had already lost the war. He realized that helping the Allies meant helping the German people. I will leave you now with these two officers. Tom will explain your assignments, and handle the logistical details. Good luck!"

At that very moment, Alex realized where he had heard the German pilot's name. He squeezed his wife's arm and pointed with his eyes at the young man.

"That's my nephew, Karl" He whispered in her ear. "I'm almost certain of this."

"Are you kidding me?" She asked, overwhelmed. "How can you be sure?"

Alex could no longer contain his emotions, and raised his hand. "Colonel Lord," he blurted in an excited tone, "before we start, I must reveal an amazing detail; this German pilot we have just been introduced to, Major Karl Kerner…he happens to be my…my nephew—the son of my late sister, Marlene. I've never met him before, not until this very precious moment!"

The room fell silent. Not a word was said. Then, suddenly, Karl cried out:

"You are my uncle, Alex Wilczek! We heard your name at home in Berlin but…"

He didn't finish his words. They fell into each other's arms, as the others applauded.

Colonel Lord said empathetically: "Let me see if I got this right: Alex, your sister married Karl's father and moved to Berlin. Frankfurt and Berlin are not that far from each other, and yet there was no connection between your families. And where do you end up meeting? Here, in the Allies headquarters in Strasbourg! I would like to congratulate you, and am convinced that you will fulfill your tasks with even greater dedication than we believed possible!"

The group parted with the Colonel and moved to the next room, to continue discussing their tasks.

The Müllers and the Wilczeks immediately liked each other and felt a deep connection, as they had chosen a similar path for their survival and freedom.

When they were done with the meeting, Alex and Erica invited the others to their room for some tea and a friendly chat.

In the Wilczeks' room, Karl was the first to speak.

"The last time I was home in Berlin," he said, "my sister, Elsa, told us that she had met you, and even visited your home, but then you suddenly disappeared. What happened to you?"

"It's a long story," Alex lowered his eyes. "We had to flee Germany."

Erica changed the subject. "Karl, tell us how you joined the Allies. It seems unbelievable!"

"After I had recovered from my injury on the Russian front, I was grounded and not allowed to fly anymore," Karl explained. " I was attached to the headquarters of the Wehrmacht's 32nd Infantry Division, which was fighting at the Moselle as part of the 6th Army, under the command of General Sepp Dietrich".

"What did you do at the headquarters?" Alex asked.

"I was assigned to be the coordinator between the Luftwaffe and the Infantry and Armored corps in that region," Karl replied. "Did you participate in heavy battles?" Erica wanted to know. "We were much busier withdrawing from the Americans and the French than fighting," Karl admitted. "Their forces were superior to ours. One night we were attacked by surprise by an American force that emerged from the east. In that battle alone, we lost many lives. We were out of supplies and everything was so confusing, that some of our forces fled eastward, thinking they were going to the German border— when in fact they fell right into the hands of the Americans. We were captured during our flight attempt.

"For a full month we were on the road, moving from one POW camp to another, enduring harsh physical conditions and rough investigations, until we arrived at a camp that had an

American commander, and I asked to meet with him. I told him my military story and asked if I could join the Allied forces."

"But what motivated you?" Alex asked, confused. Karl grimaced.

"I ran away after Hitler announced that we, the German soldiers, must kill any Ally pilot we capture. This order was made to deter the Allies from bombing the German cities, but I couldn't accept such cruel and monstrous ideas, thinking what may happen to me if I get caught by the allies' forces?"

"What do you know about the battle of the Ardennes"? One of the other men in the room, Mr. Diklow, who sat quietly until then, asked him.

"From what I learned, it was Hitler's desperate attempt to break the Allies' superiority," Karl replied. "The Germans outnumbered the Allied Forces. Even now, as we speak, there are about eighty divisions advancing towards the Rhine."

"No wonder," Mr. Diklow added. "The Americans, the British and mainly the French fought and attacked the Wehrmacht with the same zeal the Germans had during their first invasion of France."

Erica and Berta Müller left the room, and went outside to swap stories of everything they have gone through since leaving Germany. The Müllers came from Munich, the cradle of the Nazi regime. Julius Müller took part in many demonstrations against the Nazi movement, which often resulted in casualties. When the Nazis assumed power in 1933, Julius hid from the SA, which was looking for him fervently. For ten whole years, until 1943, he hid in basements in and around Munich. In the last two years he convinced his wife to join him, and together they managed to escape to Switzerland and then to France, where he was saved by the Maquis (the French Resistance). But while they were saved, their family paid the price. Mrs. Müller's sister and her entire family were sent to Dachau Concentration Camp, and their fate remained unknown.

The next morning, the Wilczeks and the Müllers arrived at Major Tom's office. After exchanging pleasantries, he asked them to wait a few more days until the region across the Rhine would be completely cleaned of the German forces. In the meantime, he asked them to go to the library and learn about the history, geography, economy and demography of the areas relevant to their assignment, such as Ottenheim, Baden-Baden, Offenburg and Alsace-Lorraine.

"The more general information you have, the easier your job will be," he said.

They all went to the library except for Karl. He stayed with the American officer, who had some questions for him. Karl told him everything he knew regarding the troops' morale, about the supply routes which had been bombarded by the Allies, and about how much more the German industry was capable of producing for the army. When he was done, Major Tom thanked him and said that they would reconvene in a few days.

Karl went back to his room and lay on his bed with his clothes on. He was emotionally drained, having endured so much over the past few months. He was just a teenager when he joined the German attempts to build the "Thousand-Year Reich", as the Führer had promised, and now, still a young man, he already had the life experiences of someone much older.

He couldn't fall asleep. He had visions from the Battle of Britain, the Russian Front, Moscow, Kharkov and Stalingrad. He remembered how it felt when he realized Germany had lost. He thought of his brigade's key term: Survival. Survival of the Führer, the army, his nation, his city and his beloved family.

Karl realized the extent to which Hitler and his commanders had deluded the Germans, regarding their ability to face the American power and potential. That was one of the main reasons for Germany's colossal failure.

Karl thought about his home, his father and his brother, the soldier, and wondered if he was still alive. He also thought about his sweet Sister, Elsa, in Frankfurt, and about his uncle Ditmar, a successful lawyer—that is, if he survived the war. Eventually, he fell asleep.

25

In the beginning of March 1945, the first units of the 9th United States Army arrived 35 kilometers away from the city of Koblenz. No one interrupted them. The same took place a few days later, as General Patton and his tanks entered Frankfurt, running into the remains of the fleeing German forces.

The group of refugees was waiting in Strasbourg for the signal to get going. At the end of March, they boarded an American jeep and headed to the town of Remagen, near Koblenz. The scenery was traumatic: they saw nothing but ruins and destruction all around them.

As soon as they entered Germany, Berta and Julius Müller jumped off the vehicle, kissed the ground and wept quietly. Even Major Tom, the tough officer, who thought he had already seen everything, was surprised by their reaction, but respected their love for their homeland.

Julius explained, apologetically: "For over two years we have been wandering throughout Europe. The longing for our country was almost too much to bear. We have been anxiously awaiting this very moment. Now, we are back home."

The rest of the group applauded and cheered.

Alex whispered in Erica's ear, "Let them do what they want, I can't see myself kissing the German ground."

"No wonder," Erica said, "you weren't born here. You're not that connected to this soil. Those who were born here and suffered so much, are now trying to find their lost world."

"Maybe you're right," murmured Alex.

Erica continued: "A regime comes and goes, but what is most important is the blood connection, and the survival of man."

"That I won't argue with," Alex smiled.

The team left Remagen and headed for Koblenz. When they arrived, on April 5th, Karl turned to a group of people on the street and asked where they could find the Town Hall.

But the people he approached seemed extremely frightened, and just stared at Karl for a few seconds. Eventually, one of them pointed at the direction of the town center, and said:

"There, where you see the American flag flying, but the building is destroyed and there is no one there."

They made their way towards the building, running into several other people on the street, but failed in starting a conversation with any of them. Then Karl had an idea. He went back to the car and returned with bread and some canned foods to give the passers-by. People began gathering around him, at first with hesitation, but then, within few minutes, the circle around them grew, until the food was all gone.

Alex said to Karl: "Look at them. They seemed completely famished, which is typical of wartime."

He then turned to one of the locals and asked him about the situation in the city and about the army's presence. The man seemed surprised by the good German but replied:

"The German Army left the city. We are here because we have no place to go. But there is nothing here but destruction. No one seems to be in charge, there are no municipal services, we have gangs breaking into houses and taking whatever is left, and we are running out of food."

The man suddenly stopped talking as he managed to get his hands on an open, almost empty can of beans that was rolling on the ground, and started licking the remains of its content from his fingers. Alex was shocked, realizing the horrible situation people lived in: hunger, devastation and misery. That man would have eaten the can too, Alex thought to himself.

Major Tom approached, and Alex said decisively that they had nothing to do in that place, and that it would be better to continue to Frankfurt, because the Germans were withdrawing eastwards, with General Patton's forces on their tail.

A short while later, the group departed for Frankfurt. On their way they witnessed the full tragedy of Nazi Germany: devastated towns and villages, bombarded bridges and a completely destroyed Autobahn system. What would usually take about 90 minutes turned into a 5-hour journey. They drove on destroyed roads, full of holes left by the bombs. They couldn't enter Frankfurt. The Americans soldiers blocked their entrance due to the ongoing battles. Major Tom decided they would spend the night in a nearby town, Königstein.

That town was also in ruins. As they neared a partially-destroyed house that seemed deserted, the front door suddenly burst open and two young children, a boy a girl, ran outside. They noticed the group and tried to get away. The boy ran very fast, looking back to see if his sister was behind him, but the girl tripped and fell right into Erica's arms. She started screaming: "*Lassen mich bitte*!" (Leave me alone, please!)

Erica hugged her and said "*Du darfst keine Angst haben, wir warden dir nicht schaden*" (You mustn't be afraid, we won't hurt you).

The girl relaxed a bit. When the boy saw that his sister was speaking to those strangers, he ran back and joined them.

Erica took a chocolate bar out of her pocket, and divided it between the two children. They hesitated but eventually took it.

"My name is Erica," Erica said and turned to the boy. "Are you her brother? What's your name?"

The boy burst into heartbreaking tears.

"My name is Hubert, and this is my sister Hansi. Our house was bombed. Our mother and grandmother are still inside. We were going out to get some help, but there is nobody left in all of Königstein."

The boy kept crying, but his sister was busy eating the chocolate bar, as if the whole thing has nothing to do with her.

Erica walked towards the open door, and the others followed her. As she stood by the entrance, she cried out loud "Is anybody home?"

At the end of the corridor, on the right side, she saw the sky through a hole in the ceiling. Apparently, a bomb had fallen into the room and destroyed it. Erica and Karl walked over, when they heard a weak groan:

"Help, please help me! Hubert, Hansi, where are you? Help me, save me, for God's sake!"

Erica and Alex went into the room. Among the debris, dust and soot, they witnessed a difficult scene. On one side of the room lay a young woman, crying and coughing. On the other side, an older woman was on the ground, motionless. The young woman stretched her hand towards Erica. She was trying to say something but could hardly utter a word.

"Where are my children, Hubert and Hansi? And where is my mother?!

Erica touched her forehead, trying to soothe her.

"Madam, your children are here," she said, and called them over. "Here they are, safe and sound, Madam."

Only then did she notice the woman's condition: One leg was completely shattered, and her face and arms were full of blood, as was her bed. The ceiling must have collapsed on her during the air raid.

Erica asked Alex to call an ambulance and bring the first aid kit from their car. She started tending to the woman, trying to stop her bleeding and ease her pain. Their driver, Moritz, came inside and explained that there was no ambulance to be found but he was told that a paramedic would be there within half an hour.

While the children stood by their mother's bedside, Erica went to check on the other woman. She saw that her skull was crushed. She went back to the younger and asked her:

"Is that woman there your mother?" "Yes," came the reply.

"She has a serious head injury. I tried moving her but she didn't respond. I'm afraid she is no longer with us."

Hearing Erica's last words, the young woman burst into bitter tears.

"Oh mother, what will I do without you?" "Where is your husband"? Erica asked

"My husband?" The woman answered bitterly. "I haven't received any information about him in a year. Perhaps he was killed on the Front, or even in one of the occupied countries. Who knows? This madman, Hitler, took all those young men and killed them."

Erica moved away from her and said to Karl: "Did you hear that? Hitler is now a madman, I'm sure now she believes this, even if three months ago she thought differently."

"She's not the only one who changed her mind; most of the people here thought highly of Hitler and his actions. Who knows how they feel now," Karl replied.

At that moment, they heard a car honk from outside. A British military truck was driving down the street, approached the house and stopped next to it. The driver and a paramedic got off, walked in and asked who needed to get to the hospital. Erica nodded towards the injured young woman.

"Not without my children! please don't leave them here alone!"

Major Tom came into the room to speak with the paramedic and the driver. They explained the woman's situation to him, and suggested that the children should come along with her. He agreed and then called the regional commander to explain that they now had to assume responsibility over the children as well. "We can't let an entire family die just because they are German," he said.

The group was highly impressed by the Major's humanitarian gesture and his determination to help a family from the enemy's camp.

After the mother was taken to the hospital with her children, Julius and Alex dug a deep hole in the yard and buried the old woman there. They even placed a makeshift cross that they made from parts of broken wood on top of the fresh grave, but didn't know what to write on it.

Julius went to the entrance and saw the family's last name: Kurzfeld. He realized that was probably the name of the

husband, the deceased woman's son-in-law, but figured that would do for the time being.

After that, the two men organized a couple of rooms in the back of the house, which weren't damaged. One of the rooms was apparently the couple's bedroom, as it was decorated with photos of their wedding and children. On their bedside table stood a photo of the husband, smiling in his Wehrmacht uniform. Karl picked it up and looked at the backside, reading the inscribed dedication:

"To my beloved wife, Margaret, from your loving husband, who is still holding on at the Front. Alfred, Bordeaux/France, May 1944".

Karl realized that May 1944 was only a month before the Allies landed on the coast of Normandy. If the man was there during the invasion, did he survive? Was he wounded or a prisoner of war? Or was he dead?

Alex called him to join the group in another room. They made themselves a meal from American military field rations, accompanied by a bottle of fine French wine they found in a closet. Afterwards, they split for the night into two rooms, men and women separately.

The next morning, Major Tom returned from the hospital and delivered the good news:

"Mrs. Kurzfeld was operated on and is out of danger. Both her legs are now in a cast. Her children are with her. We have fulfilled our moral duty, as human beings."

The others thanked him for the update. He then added: "I am also happy to tell you that Frankfurt had been liberated by the Allies; the German General, von Roth, surrendered and a ceasefire was announced. In two hours, we are leaving for Frankfurt."

They all cheered happily and Erica, with no hesitation, kissed Tom and said excitedly, "This is the best piece of news you could have possibly brought us. We are all very grateful, major."

26

Traffic on the way to Frankfurt was not very heavy, as the French and American forces had already entered. Along the way, the team members realized that their assignment of understanding the nation's morale and gathering information from the civilian population was actually redundant. The Wehrmacht had practically ceased to exist, at least in that region, and all the locals they met were just empty shells, whose world had collapsed and whose only concern was how to get food.

Alex and Erica discussed their hesitations with their friends, the Müllers. They wondered if they should retire from the mission, which had hardly even begun. As they entered the city suburbs, they decided to consult Major Tom. After all, they didn't want to disappoint him, and knew that the Americans and British helped them beyond expectation throughout their entire escape route from Sweden.

At first, Tom was surprised, but after giving it some thought, he said:

"You might be right. Due to the circumstances, this assignment had ended before it had the chance to begin. Alright, I release you from this commitment, and wish you a happier life after the war. Take Karl with you, I will discharge him as well. We've gone through a lot together. We all understand what happened to a nation that blindly followed a crazy, megalomaniac leader. Go in peace, and may God watch over you wherever you are."

During that time, Karl was looking for his sister in another quarter of Frankfurt. He saw many young men of recruitment age, wearing civilian clothing, and wondered why they weren't in the army. He asked a couple of them and they replied they had defected, threw their uniforms to the garbage and stole civilian clothing from deserted stores. In fact, they stole anything they could. Karl deduced that this phenomenon, which he had witnessed for the very first time, really marked the end of the Third Reich.

When he returned to the group, Karl was told he was a free man, with no commitment to the Anglo-Americans, and obviously not to the Führer either. The Wilczeks invited him and the Müllers to join them at their home.

They walked from Karlstrasse, through Hamburger Allee, and then along the Main River to Ouhlandstrasse, their old street. Many of the buildings they passed on their way were severely damaged by the bombings, but Frankfurt did not turn into a ghost town and even had a few neighborhoods that remained unharmed.

This was not the case for Wilzceks' neighborhood. When they arrived at their building and saw the destruction, Erica burst into tears. Alex put his hand on her shoulder and said:

"Darling, there is no point in crying. It's only four walls. We have traveled over 2,500 kilometers, and came back home safe and sound. Everything else is replaceable and repairable."

Erica couldn't come to terms with what she saw. She walked carefully through the debris to what had previously been their bedroom. Their wedding photo still hung on the one wall which remained intact, its glass frame broken. She took it off the wall and brushed the dust off. Then she removed the broken glass and put the photo in her bag. Alex followed her around with a look of deep sorrow on his face.

"We apologize that we can't host you at our home," he said to their friends. "We didn't expect such devastation. Yet, it's nothing in comparison to what others had gone through."

The rest nodded in understanding. Alex continued:

"I suggest that we all go to the US army's canteen near the train station. Hopefully, we'll be able to get a hot meal there, and then we can try to think of what to do next."

The canteen was crowded with soldiers, but no civilians. Alex came up with a wise idea, to show the staff the certificates Major Tom had given them. That enabled them to come inside and eat a good meal.

Afterwards, they sat down on a bench near the empty train station. It was the first week of liberation and there was no place to travel to, and also no means of transportation.

The group sat down and tried coming up with different ideas. The Müllers wanted to go back to Munich, but it was impossible as the city had not yet been liberated. Then Alex had another thought, and said:

"Friends, I suggest we go back to our neighborhood. I am certain we will be able to find a building that is still standing, where we can spend the night. Tomorrow will be a new day and we'll make new decisions."

Everyone agreed, and so they turned back, walking along the devastated streets. They checked every house and building and eventually knocked on the front door of an apartment building close to theirs, which appeared to be in good condition.

An older woman cracked the door open. Noticing the group, she thought they were American or British soldiers. Fearful, she began yelling "Go away, there's nobody here! Go!"

Very gently, they moved her aside, went upstairs to the first floor and started knocking on doors. There was no answer. They went to the second floor and knocked on the doors there as well. Not a sound came from any of the apartments.

Eventually, Alex grabbed the handle of one door, which opened wide.

"Is there anybody here?" he asked.

No one answered. The others followed him inside, into a spacious apartment. It had a large living room with beautiful furniture, including a small cupboard filled with precious ceramic items. The bedroom was very spacious and rich. On the bedside table they found an envelope with the name "Fleischer" written on it, and realized it must belong to the apartment's owner. They noticed three nice rooms on the eastern side of the apartment.

Berta Müller went out to the balcony and called the others to follow her. They looked outside at the street below. It was mostly devastated. People were wandering about, looking for leftover food, clothing and perhaps even dead bodies they might be able to loot.

They stepped back inside. In stark contrast to the chaos outside, everything inside the apartment seemed so neat and organized, as if the residents had just gone out shopping and would be back in a few minutes. The group members wondered why anyone would leave such a beautiful home. Were the residents afraid of Allies, and therefore decided to flee? And if that were the case, why didn't they lock the door behind them?

In the kitchen they found canned goods, including meat, beans and peas, the brand that was supplied to the German soldiers.

There was no running water in the faucets. Karl found an empty glass carafe in the kitchen closet and told his friends that he was going outside to find some drinking water.

"I'll be back in half an hour, hopefully with water," he said.

Karl went into several of the neighboring buildings, but none had any running water, and all the pipes were dry. In the sixth building he noticed a small puddle by a door which led to a storage room. *Perhaps I'll be lucky*, he thought as he opened the door, but was again disappointed not to find any pipes or faucets in the room.

He went upstairs to the first floor and knocked on the first door he saw.

"It's open, come in," a woman's voice came from inside.

Karl opened the door and found himself inside a living room, where a young woman was sitting and knitting.

"Ludwig, it's for you," she was speaking so someone in the other room. "I knew the soldiers would come and get you eventually."

A terrified-looking man, wearing a uniform and major shoulder marks came out of the room with his hands over his head. He was so terrified that he didn't even notice that the visitor, supposedly a soldier who had come to arrest him, was wearing civilian clothing.

"I know you have been looking for me for weeks," he said to Karl, "but I couldn't take it anymore. My wife is sick and she was all alone at home, so I defected. I know I committed treason. I am willing to be punished."

Karl was stunned. He thought that the man was either unaware of what was going on in the outside world, or that he had lost his mind.

"Major, I didn't come to arrest you," Karl said. "I am also a major, in the Luftwaffe. Put your hands down and take off your uniform. You are free. There is no army anymore. The Wehrmacht was defeated. The nightmare is over and you are free to take care of your wife. We don't have to account to anyone anymore".

The man looked at Karl in surprise. He didn't seem to grasp the meaning of what he was told. After a minute or two, he jumped up, grabbed Karl's hands and kissed them, then hugged him and started crying.

"I am free? We are free?!" he kept asking. "And there is no Wehrmacht, no Gestapo and no SS?"

Karl nodded.

The man was so excited that he shouted "Heil Hitler" out of habit, but quickly realized that he had made a mistake and apologized profusely:

"Excuse me, I'm sorry, that's the education we have received for twelve years. Please forgive me, say you have forgiven me!"

"I understand you," Karl said in a calm voice. "I am also the product of the same education system. Now go and soothe your wife; everything is alright."

Karl was about to leave when he remembered why he had come in the first place. He went to the kitchen closets and found six bottles of the fine Chateau Monfort wine, and six bottles of sparkling water. He decided to take all the bottles and handed the man a five Sterling note. The man refused to take the money. "The news you brought us is worth one thousand bottles! May God be with you, and may you always be well." He then walked

Karl to the door and hugged him again.

When Karl returned to the group with the bottles, they all burst into tears of joy. They laughed and raised a toast. Alex then stood up and looked out at the quiet, starry night. His mind wandered to the days before the war. *All of those lost years that went down the drain, and for nothing*, he thought to himself.

At ten o'clock, they pushed a chair against the door, so that no one would be able to surprise them at night. They fell sound asleep, the women in one room and the men in the other.

The next morning, they all gathered in the living room to discuss their next step.

Alex was the first one to speak. "We are considering staying in Frankfurt and rebuilding our lives. This is our home. We don't want to go anywhere else. At the train station, we saw bulletins explaining that the Americans are organizing a local authority here in order to restore the city. It might not be the time just yet, but I'm planning on taking my revenge on those who made me flee my beloved city. I remember every single one of those anti- Semitic snitches, and I swear, they will pay."

Berta and Julius then announced their own decision.

"We want to go back to Munich. We'll take the train as soon as it starts running again, or the bus, perhaps even today. We have some British pounds left and we think that sum is enough to cover our travel expenses. We hope we will manage once we are back in our city."

"Karl," Alex turned to his nephew, "what do you intend on doing? Would you like to join us, and together we will try to find Elsa?"

"I actually thought about doing this on my own, but I believe we'll have more success if we join forces. Moreover, you are locals and know your way around the city."

The Wilczeks and the Müllers had a tearful goodbye, hugging each other for a long time. They promised to resume contact as soon as possible.

Major Tom's group, which had originally taken upon itself the important mission of gathering information for the Allies, had dispersed. Its members were now going their separate ways.

27

Alex, Erica and Karl went back to their home on Ulhandstrasse, in an attempt to salvage some of their belongings, and perhaps even manage to renovate the place.

They entered through the back door and realized that the damage in the back was not as extensive as in the front. One of the bedrooms and the kitchen were almost intact. The beds were full of dust but that could easily be cleaned. Erica began cleaning and Alex went to fix the lock on the back door. The closed-off balcony behind the kitchen was intact as well, except for one hole in the wall, right below the ceiling. Alex decided that Karl could sleep there, but then he remembered that he hadn't checked if there was water in the pipes. He went to the bathroom, and turned on the faucet; yellowish-brownish water came out, but at least they had water!

Alex hurried to the kitchen, where the water had the same color. He turned on the faucet and let the water run for half an hour, until the color changed and became clearer. Alex began dancing for joy right there in the kitchen.

"Nothing like a war to remind you to be grateful for what you have," Karl said with a smile.

They had lunch at the American canteen, tasting Coca-Cola for the first time in their lives. Then, they decided to start looking for Elsa. Alex knew where to go first.

"In 1941 she used to work for a government office," he explained. "Until we left Frankfurt, at the end of that year, I saw her there at least twice."

"Where is it located?" Karl asked.

"On Hermannstrasse," Alex replied. "And if we don't receive reliable information there, we'll go check with your father's friends, Otto and Anna Stiebel, who live on Staufenstrasse, near our beautiful park, Palmengarten."

Elsa's office building was locked. They stood outside, banging on the gate, but no one replied. Then they headed to the Stiebels' residence.

Otto Stiebel opened the door. Alex was speechless when he saw him. Not only did he look much older than he remembered, but he also seemed broken, like a man who lost everything.

"Do you remember us?" Alex asked. "We are the aunt and uncle of your resident, Elsa Kerner. We are looking for her and wish to know how and where she is. This here is her brother, Karl," Alex said.

Otto wiped his forehead, trying to remember the people in front of him. Suddenly, his face brightened up with a smile, and he embraced Alex and kissed Erica's hands.

"Oh God! Of course, you are Alex and Erica Wilczek! What happened to you? where did you disappear to?"

"We have so many stories. But first, can you tell us if you know anything about Elsa and her whereabouts?"

"I've been yearning to meet a friendly face!" Otto said with excitement. "Please, come in! Don't stand at the door like strangers! I have to apologize, my wife won't join us—she is not ill, but is traumatized. She's been that way since a massive, one- ton bomb fell in our street, only thirty meters away from her. She was buried under the rubble. Miraculously, she wasn't physically hurt but has been in a state of post trauma ever since; she keeps imagining bombs falling around us all the time. She

can hardly function. I would have never believed that a bomb could cause this nightmare."

"Mr. Stiebel", Karl attempted to comfort him, "I've seen this phenomenon during the war, when soldiers become indifferent and apathetic and it is impossible to communicate with them. I believe it's called 'mental apathy'; the mind isn't giving the body orders on how to react to situations. It can be cured by a counter- shock. In the case of your wife, that means exposing her again to the deafening sound of a bomb falling and buildings crashing."

"Maybe this will pass by itself," Otto said bitterly, "But who knows when. Ms. Erica, please go inside her room to see her. It might jog her memory."

The two walked into Anna Stiebel's room, and found her lying on her bed with her eyes wide open, staring into space.

"Anna, my dear, look who has come to see you, Elsa's aunt and uncle. You certainly remember the beautiful young lady who once lived with us."

Otto waited for a moment, but since his wife remained in her catatonic state, not acknowledging she had even heard him, he left her with Erica and joined Alex and Karl in the living room.

"My dear friends," he said, "Elsa left Frankfurt at the end of November or the beginning of December 1944, and returned to Berlin. A month prior to her departure, she told us that her father had asked her to come home because he was all alone in Berlin and wasn't coping well with the air raids. He was desperate, couldn't sleep at night, and threatened to commit suicide if she didn't come home. We realized that he was going through something very serious, but also noticed something else: it seemed as if Elsa was also going through a crisis of her own."

"What kind of crisis?" asked Karl, worried.

"I have no idea," Otto replied. "We didn't want to pry and ask her about her personal life, but she was very nervous, and when we did ask something, she just said that everything was fine and changed the subject."

"Well, this still doesn't mean anything," Karl said.

"Once, I think it was mid-October," Otto continued, "a fancy car stopped by the front door and Elsa got out, slammed the door and ran inside the house. In addition, during her last week here, intense air raids had begun. One morning, she told us she had decided to return home immediately. We wished her luck and asked her to give our warmest regards to her father. We haven't heard from her since. To this day, I have no idea what the reason for her hasty departure was—which also took place only a few days before my Anna's tragedy."

Karl thought that if their father had said such serious things to Elsa, then his condition was indeed very bad. He considered going back to Berlin but knew the city was still out of bounds, surrounded by fighting, fire and smoke.

"Come with me," Otto interrupted his thoughts. "Let's go into her room, maybe you will find something there that can shed some light on her departure, or something you would like to take with you."

Elsa's room was tidy and neat. In one of the drawers Karl found a picture of their family from 1938; Their parents, Marlene and Franz, Elsa and himself standing beside them, and at their feet, sitting on a stool, their brother Helmut, holding a Mercedes toy car he got as a gift. Karl looked at the picture for a while and felt a pinch in his heart as he realized how beautiful his mother had been, and how good it was when the family was all together. He

missed those days which will never return, and his close-knit family.

Otto took the photo from his hand and looked at it.

"We didn't notice this photo. Had we seen it, we would have sent it to Elsa."

Karl asked for an envelope, slid the photo inside and tucked it into his shirt pocket.

Erica then came out of Anna's bedroom, with an announcement:

"I can swear Anna reacted slightly to me," she said with excitement. "She was staring at the ceiling blankly, but when I called her name, she asked me who I was. I told her but she didn't remember. It happened twice in twenty minutes. I suggest you take her to the park, so she can listen to the birds and feel the warm sun on her skin."

Karl, Erica and Alex returned home silently after their sad visit to the Stiebels. They grabbed something to eat from the leftover cans. Exhausted and disappointed, they went to bed.

During the night, they didn't hear any bombings, which meant that the fighting was withdrawing even further away.

The next morning, Alex asked Karl if he wanted to join him. "If you have no plans for this morning, please come with me; I have another matter to attend to in Nordenstrasse, uptown. The bureau in charge of supervising my company's human resources was there—but in fact, it was a secret branch of the Nazi party. I believe that Gestapo agents were there as well."

"Alex," Erica interrupted the conversation, "You are looking for Peter Hansen, aren't you?"

"Exactly, my dear. I'm not sure I'll find him. Wait for me here, and I'll be back in an hour or two," he said.

"I'm coming with you," Karl decided. "We will do this together".

On their way, Alex explained to Karl how Peter Hansen came after him when he was working at the food supply company, and the manipulative tricks he used against him. "If I had a gun,

I would shoot him on the spot," he said bitterly.

They arrived at Nordenstrasse and quickly found the building, but to their dismay, it was almost entirely destroyed by the shelling, like all the other buildings around.

"The hell with that," Alex mumbled. "You can't find anything in this rubble."

They returned to the city center. As they turned the corner to Humboltstrasse, Alex suddenly stopped and pulled at Karl's sleeve, pointing to a group of men a few meters away. Trembling, he asked Karl:

"Do you see these men? Look at the one in the middle, wearing a blue coat over a bluish sweater, the one facing us."

Alex couldn't take his eyes off the man. He was thinner, with a yellowish complexion—probably from not seeing any sunlight for a long time, and his gestures were hesitant, but no doubt: it was Peter Hansen.

Alex took a deep breath an approached him.

"Good morning, Mr. Hansen! Surely, you remember an old friend!".

"No, I don't," replied the man. "Who are you, sir?" "Look closely. I'm sure you will recognize me!" "Not at all, I don't!"

At that moment, Alex raised his palm and slapped the man angrily, with all his might and rage. The man was utterly

stunned. After a moment, he pulled himself together and called out for help.

Two Canadian soldiers, who were patrolling the area, came quickly to see what was going on.

Alex turned to them in English and pointed at the man he had just hit.

"Arrest this man. He is a Nazi, and had a top position in the regime, persecuting honest citizens. I was one of his victims."

One of the soldiers held Hansen by the arm and asked him for his name in broken German.

"Hans Schwartzman," he answered.

"He is lying!" cried Alex. "Search his pockets for documents."

One of the soldiers didn't hesitate, sent his hand into the man's coat pocket and took out Hansen's Nazi Party membership card, adorned with the Nazi flag and a swastika. Alex couldn't understand why Hansen would keep this in his pocket with the Allies in control of the city, but he didn't have a long time to reflect on the matter. The soldier whistled and a military jeep immediately appeared. Two soldiers got out and took Hansen with them.

The people on the street looked at the entire scene with indifference.

"Alex, I'm proud of how you handled this whole situation," Karl said. "Even as a soldier, I don't think I could have done a better job. Good for you!"

"That's the least I could do," Alex said with pride.

"Did you notice the people's indifference? It's as if they didn't care at all. They didn't express any resistance, and seemed perfectly compliant with the situation."

"Well, I'm glad the Canadians found out the truth. I hope he will finally get what he deserves—a long imprisonment," Alex said.

On their way home, they saw a hot-dog stand, subsidized by the Allies. Alex bought four '*frankfurters*' and brought them home, to make Erica happy.

"What do you intend to do now?" Alex asked Karl, as they were devouring the food back home.

"I am very anxious to know how my father is doing, what's going on with Elsa and, of course, with Helmut. I have no way of getting any information about them right now. Also, I want to know what's happening on the front—I don't even know where it is these days."

"You're right," Alex continued Karl's thoughts. "The German broadcasts are interrupted so often, and I haven't been able to listen to the BBC or Voice of America."

"Let's try again," Karl suggested, switched on the old radio and started turning the dial. All they got was a hissing sound, interrupted by a few musical notes here and there. He continued turning the dial, and suddenly they could hear the BBC broadcaster saying clearly:

"Here is the news summary of the last week, for our European listeners."

Alex, Erica and Karl came closer to the radio, to listen carefully.

"A week ago, on April 14th, the siege of Field Marshal Model's forces in the Ruhr area was completed. Our forces advanced quickly towards the Elbe River, on the way to Berlin. I repeat: The road to Berlin is open."

Alex, Erica and Karl jumped up and down and hugged with excitement.

The broadcaster continued: "Two days ago, we liberated the following cities: Bremen, Hamburg and Lübeck, by the Baltic Coast. On April 16th, the American forces entered the city of Nuremburg and then continued to Munich. That same day, the forces of General Zhukov launched a massive attack from the Oder river towards Berlin.

"And now, an announcement for those who have not yet been freed from the Nazi regime: Hold on! Please, remain in shelter! We are coming to liberate you."

The three were excited. Karl said, "It seemed as if the High Command of the Wehrmacht had lost control. If the news is reliable, then most of the German territories are now occupied by foreign forces."

He stood up, looked through the window at the blue, end-of-April skies, and said decisively:

"Friends, I've made up my mind. I'm heading for Berlin. The roads haven't been completely cleared yet, but I'll get as close as possible. I'll go from here to Weimar and then to Leipzig. It's only 230 kilometers. And from Leipzig to Berlin, it's another 140 kilometers."

"How are you going to make your way up north?" Alex wondered.

"I'll find the best way to advance, taking into consideration the dangers I might face," Karl smiled. "I can manage in English very well. If I'm lucky, in a week or so I'll be hugging my family."

"I understand that you have made up your mind, but can we still dissuade you from doing it right now?" Alex asked.

"Well, if you agree, I'll stay here for two more days, and leave then."

"In that case, why don't you wait another full week? The combats will surely be over by then" Erica suggested.

"I can't. I am going crazy sitting here doing nothing, not knowing what's happening with my family. Don't worry, I am a soldier and I plan on joining the Allied forces and entering Berlin with them," Karl explained. "And besides, I owe an old flame a visit. I gave her my word, that I would come find her as soon as possible."

Karl was hopeful and optimistic about the future. He had no idea what was actually going on in Berlin at the time.

Two days later, Karl kissed his aunt and uncle goodbye and left Frankfurt for Apolda. Right before leaving, Alex reminded him that just a few days earlier, the Germans celebrated the 56th birthday of their idol, Hitler. "Want to bet he won't be celebrating the next one?" Karl said.

"I will lose such a bet for sure," replied Alex, and hugged his nephew again.

Karl promised to return for a visit, with his father and siblings, once the war is over.

About fifty people were standing on the main road, trying to get a ride with any vehicle that was leaving Frankfurt. Most were German citizens who wanted to take advantage of the fact that the battles in Frankfurt had ended in order to try and get back to their home towns.

However, most vehicles were military ones, and they wouldn't take civilians with them.

Karl understood what he had to do, and moved away from the others. Some 20 minutes later, a military truck stopped next to him. The officer sitting in the front passenger seat said that they were driving to Weimar, asked Karl where he was going. Karl replied, in a good English, that he wanted to get to Berlin, through Weimar.

"I know this road very well. I did my basic training in this area. The way you're going is good for me."

The officer was intrigued by Karl's answer and asked: "Did you serve in the Wehrmacht?"

"In the Luftwaffe. I was a fighter pilot. After the defeat in the Ardennes, I was captured by the Americans and joined the Allies as a local advisor."

Karl showed him the service documents he had received from Major Tom, prepared exactly for incidents like this one.

"This is a proof that I have volunteered to help you with everything possible. As a native German, I can get inside information better than you can," Karl explained.

Karl's words left the British officer open-mouthed. The language he used and his clear explanations were very persuasive. The officer concluded that Karl was trustworthy. He told him that he had to be in Weimar by ten o'clock the next morning.

"The Nazis built a concentration camp there, Buchenwald.

Have you ever heard about it?"

Karl nodded, "I know some vague details, but they might be inaccurate."

The British officer then introduced himself. His name was Frank Stone, and he was a medical doctor who served at an international committee whose aim was to examine the results

of keeping thousands of people in the sub-human conditions of the camps for years.

"Since you are a local and speak the language, are you willing to help me?" Stone asked Karl.

"In what way?"

"You can help me coordinate the committee's work in Buchenwald. It isn't confidential work, on the contrary—what happened there should be revealed to the world, so everyone will learn the truth about the Nazi regime. What do you say?"

While that was indeed an attractive offer, Karl stalled and didn't reply right away. For him this would be a good opportunity to learn about the frightening Nazi machine. During his military service, he had heard a great deal about the Nazi atrocities, but was never presented with any proof.

The Englishman seemed to guess his thoughts. "Where are you from?" he asked.

"From Berlin. I was born there and my entire family is still there. That's why I'm going there, to see them," Karl answered.

"Come on, join me, and then you will be able to continue to Berlin," Stone suggested. "It's quite possible that, by the end of this assignment, the ceasefire will have reached Berlin. The Russians have thousands of cannons spread around the city in order to break the German military resistance. They are bombing the city non-stop."

Karl finally agreed. He was worried about his family, but understood the situation.

"There is no point in trying to enter Berlin right now, so I'll join you and get there later."

"You have come to the right decision," the officer encouraged him.

They were driving fast, passing many other military vehicles on their way. They passed the city of Apolda, and Karl reminisced about going through his basic training there, in 1940. He told the driver to take a shortcut to Eisenach, which would save them almost 300 kilometers.

They arrived in Eisenach at 5 pm, and drove to a villa that was confiscated by the Allies and used as the town headquarters. It belonged to a wealthy man who had fled Germany. Karl would finally get to sleep in a clean bed with fresh linens.

They went to the canteen for dinner. As they sat there, Karl took out the documents he had been given by Major Tom, and thanked the man in his heart. Those documents opened doors for him that no other German citizen would have been able to enter—especially not a Wehrmacht officer.

The British officer looked at him as he examined the documents.

"Mr. Kerner, can I ask you a personal question?" "Call me Karl, please."

"Alright, Karl, I have a question, but you don't have to answer it." "Please, ask me," Karl was intrigued.

"How does a German officer feel, now that the army he belonged to until recently is so overwhelmingly defeated? After all, your homeland is drowning in rivers of blood."

Karl was very surprised by the question. He paused for a

moment, pondering. Should he tell the truth or just give Stone some evasive answer?

"Look," he finally said, "I'll be honest with you. I come from a mixed family: my father is a pure Aryan, and my mother was Jewish, from Poland. We learned this about her only two years ago. Until then, no one but our father knew the truth. My mother passed away without telling us, and our father didn't reveal the secret to avoid any irreversible damage this information might have caused us."

The British officer, who by then had heard rumors about the horrors the Jews have gone through in Europe, said nothing.

Karl went on: "I served on the Moscow and Kharkov fronts. I was wounded, and after my recovery I was annexed to the brigade in the Western Front, where I fought against your forces. I know one thing; after fighting for four and a half years, I've come to realize that our attitude towards the occupied nations was abnormally bad. I was deeply and mentally broken by this realization."

Karl stopped for a moment and then continued: "I also realized that the war's objectives, as well as the means to achieve them, were completely wrong. Nothing can justify the atrocious and tragic results. Not only that: I heard that after Hitler's assassination attempt, on July 20th 1944, a top-secret order came from the main Headquarters: to execute 20 generals, 30 colonels and 100 officers of lower ranks, on charges of treason. That was Hitler's revenge. When they were drafted to the army, they swore loyalty to the Führer and to the Third Reich—but they must have felt that their nation was about to be doomed and wanted to prevent that.

"When I heard this story, I swore to myself that I would leave the Wehrmacht the first chance I had—that happened when I was captured by the Allies.

"That's understandable" the officer said in a very dry, British tone.

Karl couldn't stop.

"I saw, with my own eyes, how German guards took Russian prisoners to allegedly work in the fields, and then put a bullet through the back of their heads. What they did to the Jews in the territories they occupied—that's another horrifying chapter, and we'll see the results in Buchenwald." Karl was emotional, his eyes filling with tears.

They sat quietly for a moment. Karl's confession left Stone speechless. He heard about the tortures and the mass murders, but this was the most powerful testimony he had come across.

"I have to digest what you have just told me. It's shocking. We had no idea such atrocities took place in Nazi Germany."

That night, in his clean bed, Major Frank Stone felt that something terrible had taken place over the six years of war in Europe. He acknowledged that Karl's testimony was only the tip of the iceberg, not even realizing the sights he would soon see in Buchenwald.

The next day they set off to Weimar. Due to heavy traffic on the roads, it took them an entire day to get there.

When they were close to Buchenwald, Stone turned to Karl. "Did you know that the camp we are arriving at was liberated on April 11th, just a few days ago? I read reports written by American officers, who described the atrocities committed by the camp's staff, under the authority of the SS. They mentioned that it was very difficult to grasp the scope of the horror."

"I am not surprised," replied Karl. "This only serves to intensify my own impressions."

Stone and Karl arrived at the newly-liberated camp, not yet realizing the hell they were about to encounter.

Buchenwald

28

As Karl and Stone approached the camp, they immediately noticed its pathetic-looking barracks, built on the hills north of Weimar. Stone told Karl about the city's history, and especially about the Weimar Republic, which collapsed when Hitler rose to power.

As they arrived at the camp, they saw American soldiers guarding the gates, stopping anyone who wanted to enter; only those with an official pass could get inside.

Karl lifted his eyes and saw the sign hanging over the gate:

Jedem das Seine. It sent chills down his spine. "What does this mean?" Stone asked him.

"To each what he deserves," Karl looked straight at him.

They showed their passes to one of the guards and asked where they could find Colonel Brown. The guard looked at the board on the wall and directed them towards a concrete structure some fifty meters away which was used as the camp's headquarters.

They walked over, looking at the camp around them. Nothing of what they had read or heard could have possibly prepared them for the shocking sights that appeared before their eyes. On both sides of the footpath stood human skeletons, wearing striped pajamas, and looked at them curiously as if they had never seen people before. Some gave them weak, toothless smiles. Those were not prisoners but rather human remains, skin and bones.

Stone and Karl couldn't meet their gazes.

They approached the cabin marked by a sign in English: "The International Red Cross Organization, the Investigation Committee of Nazi Crimes". Below, it stated "Colonel Samuel Brown". They knocked on the door and let themselves in.

Five tables loaded with files and reports took up most of the space in the room. Ally officers sat around the tables, examining the various documents. Stone asked about Colonel Brown and one of the officers pointed to a hall down the corridor. Brown was sitting there with two officers and another man in civilian clothing. Stone introduced himself first and then introduced Karl.

"This is Major Karl Kerner, a former Luftwaffe pilot, who defected and is now working with our forces in an attempt to save what can still be saved from his country. He is helping us investigate the crimes carried out by his former commanders."

Karl handed his papers to the colonel, who examined them very carefully.

"It's too bad we don't have thousands more like you, it would have made our job much easier!" the colonel said.

He invited them to sit down and turned to Major Stone. "Now that you are here, our committee is in full attendance

and we can get to work. Since the camp's liberation, about 6000 prisoners had already left— those whose condition, according to our doctors, was very serious. They were sent to various hospitals outside of Germany".

"What about those miserable people we saw outside?" Stone inquired.

"There are still about 17,000 people here, if you can even call them people," replied the colonel. "They are in poor health, but if we get a decent supply of food and vitamins, we will be able to

treat them here. Since we couldn't have even fathomed what would be waiting for us here at the camp, we came unprepared and now have to wait for provisions."

The colonel showed Karl and Stone the maps and diagrams hanging on the wall.

"Since 1937, when this camp was built, some 240,000 people from 30 countries were imprisoned here. Among them there were 10,000 Jews and about 8,000 Germans who opposed the regime."

He paused for a second to let them absorb this information. "About 43,000 prisoners, mostly Russians, perished. They

were either murdered or had died from starvation and various diseases. When our forces came in here, we discovered that the 4,000 Jewish prisoners who remained in this inferno suffered the most, and now we all know the reasons for that."

"Why is that?!" Karl cried out, feeling the shock take over him. "You know," said the colonel, "on my way here, I passed through Paris. I stopped at the Sorbonne University and looked into the phenomenon of anti-Semitism in occupied France. I came across posters which said: 'Tuberculosis, syphilis, and cancer can be cured—but Judaism cannot. Let us end it'. This is just one example that helps you understand the depths of hatred towards the Jews. This is a plague which has taken over Europe in its entirety."

Karl felt dizzy and sat down at the table. Stone and the colonel noticed his reaction and came to sit beside him.

The colonel held his hand and said: "I am sorry I have to burden you with all of these shocking details, but in order for you to do your job properly, you need to know the truth about this place.

"According to the documents we seized," he continued, "there were two commanders here: Karl Koch, between 1937 and 1942, and then Hermann Pister, until the camp's liberation. After 1942, ammunition factories were built near the camp, and thousands of prisoners, including about 800 Jewish women, worked there as slaves. In the winter of 1943 they were taken to the factory, and on the way back were murdered in cold blood. The main figure of this horrible story was the commander's wife, Ilse Koch.

"What was her role in the camp?" Stone inquired.

"Oh, you will hear a lot of horror stories about her during your stay here," the colonel replied. "But if we speak about the atrocities carried out in this place, I can tell you that when we arrived, there was a large group of Gypsies who served as an experimental group; they were given nothing but salt water, because the Germans wanted to find out how long they could survive. Within three weeks, half of them were dead. Only after that, did the Germans stop starving the remaining ones."

Karl felt empathy towards this American colonel, who spoke with such sorrow in his voice.

"Major Stone, you are a doctor, aren't you?" inquired Brown, and Stone answered with a nod.

"In that case, I'd like for you to prepare a detailed report of the prisoners' medical condition. A report was already prepared by the medical staff that accompanied the liberating forces, but it is far from perfect," Brown continued. "You can have anyone you'd like from the team to help you. Please, complete the report in no more than five or six days. When you're done, please show it to me first, and together we'll add whatever might be necessary. I have to hand it in to the Combined Chiefs of Staff when they meet in Paris on May 9th."

Stone thanked the colonel for his trust and asked to have another doctor and an administration officer added to his team, and of course Karl as well, who would be of great assistance as a native German.

Half an hour later, two officers came up to Stone: Lieutenant Robert Gordon, a young physician who had served in the Third Army of General Patton, and Lieutenant Dan Lloyd, an administration officer who had left Germany with his parents when he was five years old, and knew only basic German.

After dinner, they went for a tour of the camp. Lloyd told Stone that his father had developed an interest in the Nazi regime and its horrible actions, sharing with him everything he had read about Buchenwald.

"However, when I arrived here I realized we didn't know very much at all," Lloyd continued. "For example, I learned that the camp was divided into many sub-camps, which together formed three sections: the largest was allocated to the oldest prisoners, the smallest was a detention camp, and the tent camp was for the Polish prisoners, who were sent here at the end of 1939."

The group passed by the miserable-looking barracks. The prisoners were standing outside, looking at them with blank eyes. With Karl's or Lieutenant Lloyd's help, Stone asked them some questions: where they had come from, and what they were expecting from the American forces now that they were free. The prisoners' responses were confusing and incoherent. It was evident that they have not yet grasped the full meaning of their liberation.

Outside one of the barracks, two prisoners were arguing angrily. They looked less pitiful than the others. Stone approached and asked Karl to start questioning them.

"When did you arrive here?" Karl asked one of the men, who seemed about 50 years old.

"I arrived in 1944, and my friend here came in 1943," the man answered.

"Where are you from?" Karl continued.

"I am from Berlin. Excuse me, I haven't introduced myself. My name is Ditmar, and my friend here is French, from Lille. His name is Bernard Lorisson."

Karl Looked at him, and a sudden memory flash crossed his mind. *Where do I know this man from? He asked himself. His skinny face and body, the yellowish beard, his intonation...* Something seemed familiar, but he couldn't identify exactly what.

Karl decided to continue questioning the man. "You said that you are from Berlin and your name is Ditmar. I didn't catch your last name, could you please repeat it."

"Kerner, sir"

Suddenly, Karl remembered. But was this even possible? "Are you Ditmar Kerner, the Berlin lawyer, whose brother is the pharmacist Franz Kerner?"

The prisoner looked at him curiously, as did the rest of the group.

"Yes, sir, but who are you? How do you know my brother's name and profession?"

Karl approached the man and gave him a big hug. "I am your nephew, Karl, your brother's son!"

Before he could explain the situation to the group, Ditmar jumped in and began telling his own story:

"I am indeed Ditmar Kerner, the Berlin attorney. Up until six months ago, I was a high-ranking SS official. However, I was expelled from the organization and sent to this concentration camp after being accused of allegedly participating in an act of theft, which I had never committed. I have no idea if that theft had even taken place and if so, who had committed it. I only know that I was a victim of the system and its methods. I am referring to the SS, of course. I was a fool to accept the job in the organization, blinded by the good life I led in the beginning. The price I paid was great. I was convicted without a trial and sentenced to one of the worst punishments in existence. I suppose that only a death sentence is worse. You know, in hindsight, I deserved this punishment, not because I had committed a crime—I hadn't! But because I believed in this group of criminals, who have no ethics or morals. They were looking for an easy victim, and there I was."

Ditmar took in a deep breath and looked at his audience, as if he wanted to make sure they fully understood him.

"I can tell you a lot about the atrocities of Buchenwald, some of which I experienced myself, and some I have heard about from the prisoners who were here before me and disappeared," Ditmar went on ceaselessly. "Have you heard about the former commander's wife, Ilse Koch? She was a true product of the Nazi inferno. Her brutality here surpassed even the many other cruel acts that had taken place in all the other concentration camps. She was notorious for torturing prisoners to death, and for many other horrific acts. For instance, she ordered her workers to make lampshades and 'leather' bags for the officers' wives from the victims' skin. This is too frightening to even think about.

Hardly anyone survived her tortures, but I was one of the lucky few.

"In August 1944, just before the liberation of France, a group of Jews was transported from Drancy. My friend was one of them." He pointed at him and continued "Some of those poor men died on the way, in the notorious railway cars that led them here."

Right then, Ditmar burst into loud sobs. All the horrible memories he has been keeping in his heart for so long suddenly flooded him and he broke down, feeling overwhelmed. He took a piece of cloth out of his striped coat and wiped his face.

"I beg your pardon, but I can't keep these memories inside anymore. They will accompany me for the rest of my life, until my dying day," he apologized.

Karl translated everything to Stone, who meticulously wrote down all the details in his small notebook.

"Uncle Ditmar," Karl turned to him in a more personal tone, "what do you know about father and the rest of the family?"

"Nothing! We were completely detached from the external world here."

"Are you married?" Karl inquired.

"Don't you know? I am married and I have a daughter. Fortunately, my wife and daughter weren't deported to a concentration camp because my wife's father is a German nobleman, so they could remain in Berlin. But I know nothing about their fate, and it kills me. Besides, I don't know anything about the fighting. Where is the Front nowadays? I must leave this place and go find my family!"

"Uncle Ditmar," Karl stopped him, "you must be patient. Most of the prisoners here have been waiting for so long, a few more days won't matter. And anyway, you have no place to go to because we are still at war. I promise you, once the situation is better, I'll come back and take you home. Please, don't do anything foolish and don't try to escape!"

Ditmar nodded reluctantly.

In the meantime, Stone was having a chat with Lorisson, Ditmar's friend. Despite the fact that he looked like all the other prisoners, there was a different air about him. They spoke French, and Lorisson answered Stone's questions after lengthy thought.

"Mr. Lorisson, I understand that you are from Lille, and that you arrived here in 1943. Can you tell me, please, what were the circumstances under which you were deported?"

"I am a chemist," Lorisson replied. "I continued working even under the German occupation. They needed chemists to manufacture medicine for their Wehrmacht soldiers and set up laboratories in Lille. My colleagues and I went on like this until two months before we were deported."

"And then what happened?" Stone inquired.

"At that time, apart from the regular medication we were producing such as iodine, pain relievers, and various ointments and vitamins, we were ordered to start manufacturing poisons, and wrap them up in special packaging labeled 'Not for human use'. We heard many stories of how the Germans were treating their prisoners in the concentration camps, and were very concerned that our poisonous substances were used on them. Many people from our hometown were deported to those camps."

"What did you do then?" Stone asked.

"We started flushing those poisons into the toilet. Unfortunately, just then the Nazis decided to disinfect the entire lab, sewers included, and so they found out what we had done. Four of the eight people who worked in the lab, myself included, were put on trial. Three of us were deported to three different concentration camps. I have no idea what happened to my colleagues, nor to my family. I'm afraid that as a result of what I did, a terrible fate befell them."

For seven days, Stone and his team collected testimonies. They encouraged the prisoners to tell them everything they had gone through. A few days after that, Stone handed in his report to Colonel Brown. The latter read it very carefully, marking notes in the margins, especially on things pertaining to the prisoners' food, clothing and sleeping conditions.

On May 8th, 1945, the report was ready to be sent to the Combined Chiefs of Staff, who were gathering information on the concentration and death camps in Nazi-occupied Europe. That very night, the sound of bells ringing merrily was heard throughout the continent; those were the bells of freedom for the millions who had survived this war.

BERLIN IN FLAMES

29

By December 1944, the fact that the Third Reich was about to collapse was already well-known to many Germans. Elsa also felt the same, and therefore decided to go back home. She made her way from Frankfurt to Berlin anxiously, concerned about her father's wellbeing. Upon her arrival in the city, she raced to the family home and was immensely relieved to find him there.

Franz hugged her tightly.

"If you hadn't come home, I would have gone insane," he said. Elsa hugged him back with excitement, but then she suddenly noticed that he had changed. She looked into his eyes: they were lifeless. He looked like a frightened old man.

"Father, what happened to you?" she asked, horrified.

"You, Karl, Helmut were all gone. I had no information about any one of you, I didn't even know if you were alive. Being in the dark like that killed me. Nothing in this world is more precious to me than the three of you!"

Elsa caressed his head, and he burst into tears. "This is the tragedy of our people today," she said.

"We mustn't agree to that," Franz said with tears in his eyes. "My brother, Ditmar, was imprisoned by his SS colleagues and then deported to Buchenwald. Did you ever hear about that place, Buchenwald?"

"Yes," she replied. "It's a concentration camp to which opponents of the regime and wealthy Jews were deported, right?" "It's not just a concentration camp, I heard that it is hell on earth," Franz explained.

"Was Uncle Ditmar a regime opponent? I knew he was a colonel in the SS who was working with the organization's top hierarchy, wasn't that the case?"

"He was accused of stealing half a million dollars—a theft he had never actually committed!"

Elsa looked at her father with dismay.

Franz continued, "I know him very well. He has his shortcomings, and he has made many mistakes in his life, but my brother is no thief. I am certain of that. You should have heard how he spoke about the Nazi regime and of his friends there, with so much admiration."

"I remember him with the uniform and the ranks on his shoulder," Elsa said. "He was so proud. He told us about the parties at Göring's and at Dr. Funk's houses. That made him so happy."

Frank calmed down a bit, took Elsa's hand, and looked tenderly into her eyes.

"Tell me about your life in Frankfurt."

"When I stopped receiving letters from you, and the phones were disconnected due to the shelling, I went absolutely mad," she told him. "After a few months, I went to my boss, a kind-hearted man, and told him I haven't received any sign of life from my father for a while, and that I urgently required a few days off. He refused at first, until he finally agreed to let me go, under one condition—that I would take only a few days, and return to work as quickly as possible. I promised to do so. Nevertheless, I have no intention of going back. I want to stay here with you, father."

Elsa turned quiet and looked down. Franz understood there was something else she wanted to share with him.

"Elsi," He whispered, "What are you hiding in your silence?"

Elsa turned her head away from him and began crying. Franz extended his arm and stroked her hair. She turned around and said:

"Something else that happened to me in Frankfurt. About six months ago I met a man. He was older than me, about 35. I fell in love with him despite the age difference."

"Who was he?" asked Franz.

"His name was Werner von Bock, the nephew of Marshal Fedor von Bock, who fought on the Russian Front, along the Volga River. I saw many pictures at his home, with the Marshal and the entire family. He told me he was a Wehrmacht officer, but I had never seen him in uniform. He was very attractive and intelligent, a graduate of the University of Göttingen with a PhD in sociology. His thesis was titled 'Researching External Influences on Indo-European Nations in the Past 1000 Years.' I was completely dazzled".

"I can understand that. You are a young pretty woman, after all," Franz said sympathetically.

"We enjoyed our great romance for several months, and were very much in love. I increasingly understood that he was addicted to the Nazi doctrine, but never gave it a second thought. We celebrated every German victory and cried over every defeat. But more than anything, we were busy loving each other."

Elsa's voice firmed as she continued her story.

"One day, back in October, we were at his home together with one of his friends, a university professor. It was very cold outside and we were having wine to heat up. It was the day Athens was conquered by the British. That day, the newspaper editorials wrote about the drafting of all of the Reich's 'human resources', especially the youngsters. Half a million young people, between the ages 15 and 18, responded to the call for self-sacrifice. They came from high schools, workshops and their family homes, and together formed 25 new divisions.

"Werner read the editorials and said that this was the best way to show the Führer how much he was loved, but then added: 'At the core of all of our troubles and disasters you can find the Jews, the allies of the international imperialists and of those damned Bolsheviks. Himmler didn't take care of them as needed; he should have eliminated them all.' When I heard his words, I was shocked. Although Werner was a little intoxicated, I could tell it wasn't the alcohol but rather his own deep conviction that made him say those things. Since I already knew that we have Jewish blood running through our veins, I was traumatized, father. I haven't become a Jew-supporter all of a sudden, our education was different, but I love mother too much to disgrace her memory like that."

Franz looked at his daughter with pain, but said nothing.

She went on: "Besides, I didn't understand exactly what Werner's meant about Himmler not eliminating Europe's Jews." "I don't really know what he meant, but it sounds bad," Franz said and then asked her, "What did you do next?"

"I left his apartment angrily, and told him I had a bad headache," Elsa replied. "The next morning, he came to my office but I refused to see him. He continued sending me flowers and messages, asking why I was so mad. I didn't answer him. Then, a short while later, I left Frankfurt and came home, to you."

Franz was shocked by his daughter's story. He had always known that she will have a romantic affair at some point, but would have never fathomed it would turn out to be such a cruel experience for her. He gently caressed her head, trying to ease her pain.

"I loved him with all my heart, and I believed in him," Elsa whispered.

"You must forget this unsuccessful romance," her father was decisive, but his tone of voice changed and Elsa could sense he was troubled.

Elsa picked up on this. "Don't worry, mother still managed to teach me a few things about men before she died. He didn't get me pregnant."

"Thanks God!" With that affirmation, Franz could relax.

At that moment, they heard the loud noises of shelling, right by their house.

"I can't stand this anymore!" Franz said. He got up and started pacing around the room.

Elsa went over to him and gave him a hug. "Father, there is nothing we can do. All of this will be over soon."

"This is terrorism against the population, what kind of war is this?" he asked desperately.

"Father, do you remember Karl's stories about us bombing England? Now I understand them. They didn't enjoy this kind of war either. Now they are retaliating," Elsa explained.

"It feels like you're justifying their attacks," Franz said and looked out the window. He saw the bombs drop. The street was full of smoke, to the point of suffocating. There were no firefighters or rescue forces in sight.

"Where are we going to sleep tonight? We can't stay here now, and we are also running out of food," Franz said and rubbed his hand on his forehead. Elsa remembered her father made that gesture whenever he felt weak or desperate.

"Father, our house is still standing, we still have a roof over our heads," she tried to soothe him.

Franz walked over to the corner, sat down and held his head in his hands.

"May God save us," he said.

In January of 1945, Marshal Zhukov's army crossed the Vistula River and conquered Warsaw from the north, and then carried on until it was only 200 kilometers from Berlin. The Russians also conquered Prussia and arrived at Danzig.

The Americans advanced all the way to Koblenz, and Hitler instructed his army to destroy all of their military facilities and leave nothing but scorched earth behind them. In mid-April, Field Marshal Model's army surrendered. 300,000 German soldiers were captured, along with 30 generals.

The road to Berlin was finally open.

The American and Russian divisions met by the Elbe River. Additional Russian forces came into the city from the Oder. Germany was divided into two, and Hitler remained besieged in his Berlin bunker. On April 30th, he and his wife, Eva Braun, committed suicide. The following day Joseph Goebbels, the Minister of Propaganda, who had served as the Chancellor of Germany for a single day following Hitler's suicide, took his life as well, along with his wife and six children.

On May 7th, in Reims, General Alfred Jodl, Germany's Chief of Staff, signed the nation's instrument of surrender, without prior conditions. That marked the end of Nazi Germany's short, bloody history.

The massive invasion of the Allied forces, in April 1945, clarified the situation for the German people; they suddenly realized that the Third Reich had come to an end, differently from what their Führer had once promised them.

On April 3rd, two armed men dressed in khakis, with swastika bands on their right arms and a sign that read *Volkssturm Berlin*, knocked on the Kerners' front door. They asked Franz for his identity card. They examined it and then handed him an induction order, which stated that he was required to join the army within 24 hours. He was to arrive at a unit located at the Zoological Garden, near the train station.

Those men were representatives of a militia Hitler had founded in the autumn of 1944, in order to defend the Nazi elites from German officers who he suspected might rebel against him. Boys as young as 16, as well as men 55 and older, were drafted to this militia. All the others were already serving in other military units.

Franz weighed his options; he knew he couldn't join the militia at that point—that would be suicide! And yet, an order is an order.

All of a sudden, he remembered the organization "Medical Services for Civilians", which was quite helpful back in those days. Franz himself had personally helped the director of the organization three years earlier, when one of his family members required some special medicine, which Franz managed to obtain. He went to speak with him immediately, and told him that he was now the one in need.

The director was happy to help, and quickly produced a document, which stated that his organization required Franz's pharmaceutical knowledge, and that he must be present at his pharmacy every day between 8 am and 8 pm.

When the two Militia men returned, a few days later, to check on why Franz had not reported to his assigned unit, he showed them the document.

"Only a traitor is capable of avoiding serving the Nation, *Du bist ein Schwein* (you are a pig)," they shouted, and left angrily.

30

On April 20th, Hitler's birthday, Franz came home with a large metal container full of water. Finally, after many days, a tanker came to their neighborhood, and the driver gave out water to the residents. Each family received four liters. No one celebrated the Führer's birthday; people were in a state of despair, traumatized by the long war.

Half an hour after Franz returned home, there was a knock on the door, and Elsa opened it hesitantly. A skinny, wounded man stood there. Fearing the defector hunters that roamed the streets, he had removed the shoulder ranks from his dirty uniform.

Elsa looked at the pitiful man for a long moment, and then it hit her.

"Father, it's Helmut! God, he looks horrible!" she yelled.

Helmut limped inside, mumbled something about pain in his arms and legs, and collapsed.

Franz and Elsa dragged him to one of the beds, and quickly noticed that he suffered from shrapnel injuries in his abdomen and left arm. Elsa removed the dirty bandage wrapped around his arm and almost threw up; his wounds have been bleeding for what seemed to be several few days, and have become infected and full of pus? She rushed over to the medicine cabinet and took out some ether to put against Helmut's nostrils, so he would wake up.

Helmut opened his eyes and groaned in pain.

Franz and Elsa removed his clothes, washed him with a wet cloth and applied some antibiotic ointment to his wounds.

Then they changed the bandages and dressed him in clean pajamas. He kept drifting in and out of consciousness, uttering unclear words.

All of a sudden, he jumped out of the bed and screamed:

"It is an artillery shell, not a bomb! Go find shelter! Why are you standing like this?! Move!"

Then he lay down again and fell asleep.

"God knows what he has been through, but it's manifested in his nightmares," Franz whispered to his daughter.

"We should let him sleep peacefully for now," Elsa suggested. "We'll find out everything tomorrow."

Helmut slept for 24 hours. He suffered from nightmares and shouted out things like "Where are the firefighters?" or "I'm injured, can somebody help me?"

After one full day he woke up, wondering where he was and who had helped him.

"Helmut, can you hear me?" his father asked, bending over him, "If you can understand me, please blink."

Helmut blinked three times, and Franz was overjoyed.

"You are at home, my son," he said gently and caressed his forehead. "Elsa took care of you, like a real nurse."

"I am so thirsty," Helmut mumbled. "Can I get something to drink?"

Franz brought him glass after glass of water. After he was done drinking, Helmut fell asleep again. His breathing was now calm and regular. Franz felt relieved.

"Thank you, God, we'll take good care of him."

He went to the other room and asked Elsa: "Who taught you how to tend to people like that, like a nurse? I looked at you while you were treating your brother and was very impressed."

"Father, do you remember when I took that language course?"

"Of course," Franz replied.

"Well, besides languages, for two hours each week we had to learn how to treat injuries and burns. Some of my colleagues didn't take it seriously. I did, and I'm glad I did—look how helpful it turned out to be," Elsa said with a sense of pride.

The next day, 36 hours after he returned home, Helmut woke up and opened his eyes.

"Food, I want to eat something, please."

His hunger was a clear sign that he was getting better. His father and sister prepared breakfast from the leftovers they had at home. They sat by his bed while he devoured the food, not even stopping to breathe. Suddenly he stopped, and stared at his fork.

"What happened, Helmut?" His father asked.

Helmut remained quiet for some time, and then said: "I killed our sergeant."

Franz and Elsa stared at him.

"We were at Wannsee, when ten aircrafts began bombarding us. Our situation was very bad, as we had run out of ammunition. All of a sudden, I could hear the sergeant yelling at one of the soldiers: 'Why aren't you shooting, you bloody Bolshevik?!' The soldier explained that there was no ammunition left, and then the sergeant pulled out his gun, approached him and shot him in his head as he frantically screamed: 'This is how we treat any sign of disobedience!'

"We were all completely stunned. At that very moment, we felt the ground shake; a few meters away, two bombs fell from the sky. Six of our soldiers were killed on the spot. The sergeant continued yelling, trying to overcome the noise of the aircrafts. 'You see,' he said to us, 'this is coming from the Bolsheviks, the Jews and the capitalists, they are all against us'.

"When I heard those words, I approached him and looked him in the eye. I was furious. He tried to say something, but only got the chance to utter 'Sir, officer, please, no!' before I put a bullet in his throat. He fell onto the ground. Then I ordered all the others to look for shelter, and immediately turned around and walked away."

Franz and Elsa looked at each other, speechless.

"I think I was completely shell-shocked," Helmut continued. "It was a mixture of wrath and uncontrollable madness. I rushed to the main road and just started walking until I arrived home. I'm afraid they will come looking for me here. You know that there is a death penalty, without trial, for killing a soldier and leaving your post in the middle of a battle."

"What shall we do?" Franz asked in despair.

"Elsa, do you remember the basement where we used to play hide-and-seek when we were children?" Helmut asked.

Elsa nodded.

"It's a good place to hide. Could you please fix it up so I can use it?"

Franz thought that his son had committed an act of heroism, at least in his eyes: he wasn't even 21 years old, and he had the courage to kill a mad sergeant. But of course, in the eyes of the Wehrmacht, Helmut was a traitor who must be sentenced to death.

"Elsa," he ordered his daughter, "please do as Helmut has requested and swear you will never speak a word to anyone about this!"

After he was comfortably situated in the basement, Helmut continued his story.

"As you know, I was serving as an officer in the anti-aircraft artillery unit, and was stationed near Wannsee, with a parallel unit from Potsdam. Together, we formed a battalion. Our duty was to respond to attacks from the north and the west. Our staff was exceptional, but the tasks that were imposed on us exceeded our abilities. We couldn't take it anymore. The Anglo-American aerial attacks were just killing us. They came in massive waves, day and night."

Franz nodded. He didn't tell his son how it felt to experience those attacks on the home front. He let him speak and ease his burden.

"We would eat, sleep and defecate by the cannons. Life was worse than hell. We were under so much pressure, that the soldiers eventually abandoned their posts and left us, the officers, with unmanned teams. And who do you think were the ones to blame? We were, the commanders in the field. One of my colleagues, officer Schmeister, was executed right by his battery. He was blamed for disregarding the instructions simply because a few of his soldiers had fled. I was luckier. Although I was also charged, on that very day I was moved to another unit near Dresden, who had lost several of its commanders.

"The drive from Berlin to Dresden lasted a full day. We arrived on February 11th, at night. The city was beautiful, with its impressive, historical buildings. It felt like paradise, but two nights later, God's wrath came down on the city in the form of an unimaginable aerial bombardment. 35,000 people were killed, and over 50,000 were wounded."

Franz couldn't contain his shock and let out a whistle.

"A week later, we were sent back to our base in Wannsee," Helmut went on. "We were working ceaselessly, day and night, without food or sleep. Then, in March, we received the news: Reich Marshal Hermann Göring was expected to pay a visit to our unit. He arrived on the 5th of the month, and was received with all the rules of ceremony, including a military band. And meanwhile, our soldiers were dying," Helmut said dryly.

"Göring entered our commander's office, and a moment later, terrible screams were heard. He yelled at our commander: *'Wir haben den Krieg verloren'* (we lost the war) and *'Alles ist zerstört'* (everything is destroyed). Then the both of them came out to meet all the officers in the dining hall. Göring was hysterical and couldn't control himself. He pointed at us and shouted that we were the reason for the disaster Germany was experiencing.

He asked our commander, in a fury, how many enemy aircrafts we have shot down since the beginning of the month. My commander replied that we had shot down three aircrafts.

"Göring then looked at every single one of us, and began yelling frantically: 'We are attacked by hundreds of aircrafts every day, and we only shoot down three?! And who's to blame for that?! You, the lousy soldiers!' Our commander was trying to explain that we had run out of ammunition, but Göring wouldn't listen. He shouted some more, then just left the base with his entire entourage.

"We continued firing less and less anti-aircraft missiles, since very little new ammunition had arrived. Then I had that incident

I told you about, and I escaped and came back home. I am so grateful you are alive!" Helmut concluded his terrible story.

Franz patted his youngest child on his head, with tears in his eyes. He would have never imagined that was how his son would spend his youth.

31

On April 23th, 1945, the Russians arrived at the suburbs of Berlin and came face-to-face with the *Hitlerjugend*. The youngsters were drafted in haste just a few months earlier, and were quickly trained and organized into small infantry groups. They had very little ammunition, and the massive Russian divisions easily brushed them off.

The day the Russians entered Berlin, Helmut went out of his shelter to the street. Surprisingly, he bumped into his former commander, Lt. Colonel Erich Kaufmann. They fell into each other's arms, excited. Kaufmann told Helmut that he was actually on his way to look for him, because he, too, had run away from their unit, and Helmut was the only person he could trust.

"They all left, even before I did. There was no point in fighting almost alone in a practically non-existent military unit," he explained.

"We can't define it as running away. It's more of an abandonment," Helmut replied.

With a bitter smile, Helmut reminded him how, only two months before Göring's visit, Kaufmann was promoted and the entire unit was praised for its excellent work in protecting the skies of Berlin.

"Why did you desert the unit, what happened?" Helmut asked him.

"A week ago, I received the worst possible news," Kaufmann said in a small voice. "I was informed that my entire family was killed in an aerial attack that hit our house."

Helmut grabbed his hand and said nothing.

"We lived not far from here, on Hauptstrasse number 6. The entire area was reduced to rubble that day. My parents were killed on the spot, and my wife and daughter were critically injured and died two days later at some improvised local clinic," Kaufman said in an even voice, still incapable of expressing his deep pain and anger.

"To hell with the Wehrmacht, the Reich and the Führer! If in 1940, when I received a decoration of heroic valor for my part in the Battle of Dunkirk, someone would have told me this is how things will end, I would have put a bullet in his head!"

Helmut tried to calm his friend, but he couldn't stop talking. "Our daughter was an angel. Only thirteen, and already

playing Beethoven and Mozart on her violin. She was a virtuoso, and I will never forget how much she loved music. Listening to her play was a wonderful experience."

Kaufman began sobbing, and Helmut put his arm around his shoulder.

"What will I do now? I have nowhere to go! Yesterday, I buried them all in my back yard, because I had no way of taking them to the cemetery. There is no way I can go back to that house!" he was now weeping like a child.

"Come home with me," Helmut suggested. "Miraculously, our house is still in one piece."

At that moment, a massive Russian artillery attack began. Shells fell heavily all around them. Helmut dragged his friend

underneath a concrete awning, which provided some sort of shelter.

When the attack was over they rushed back to Helmut's home, where he introduced Kaufman to his father and sister, and briefly told them about what had happened. Franz, feeling a wave of empathy towards the poor man, hugged him warmly and said:

"We are all the victims of our country, my dear friend."

The attack on Berlin lasted for several days and nights. Thousands of bombs landed in the already-devastated city. Smoke filled the air and hid the sunlight. Small Russian units broke into houses and demanded alcohol, women and watches. When rumors of the brutal rapes the Russian soldiers were committing began to spread, Franz, Helmut and Kaufmann didn't hesitate for a moment. They gathered wood from the rubble around them and thickened the walls of the basement where Helmut had hidden. Now, it was Elsa's turn to hide there. They weren't overreacting. In the early hours of May 1st, three drunk Russian Soldiers broke into the house. It seemed they were cheerfully celebrating International Workers' Day. The senior member among them, an officer, waved his rifle at them and yelled: "Davai (come on, give) alcohol, vodka and Frauen (women)!"

"We have no women here," Franz replied, signaling "no" with his hands.

The Russians brutally pushed him aside and started looking through the house. Since they couldn't find any women, they demanded the men's watches. Franz, Helmut and Kaufmann removed the watches from their wrists and handed them over.

The Russians took them and left the house, to look elsewhere for poor women they could rape.

The neighborhood residents were terrified. They sought shelter in the sewer system, the train tunnels and old bunkers. One of the elderly men who lived on the street suggested that a few of the young women volunteer to give themselves to the Russians, in order to satisfy them and save the others.

When the bombardment ceased for a while, five brave women came out of their hiding places and walked out to the street. When the Russians saw the women, they dragged them into a partially-ruined structure, where they raped them brutally, like animals, for hours and hours.

"Now I understand why they say that if you are captured, make sure to fall into the hands of the Americans and not the Russians," Helmut told Kaufmann as they looked at the young women leave the structure, looking like empty shells of their previous selves.

"Our soldiers did the same in France and Russia," Kaufmann said. "And they did more than just rape the women: they also murdered them and their husbands, if they were at home at the time."

Helmut was speechless. Despite everything he had gone through, he still had some innocence left in him.

"I'm sorry to ruin your illusion, but the conqueror acts the same way, regardless the flag he is fighting for," Kaufmann said. "In Dunkirk, I saw with my own eyes how our soldiers gathered all the young women in the center of town, chased the men away, and then raped them. I would prefer to forget what they had done to them, and how those poor women screamed in an attempt to save themselves. This here is the Russians' retaliation."

That same day, May 1st, a rumor quickly spread through Berlin, saying that Adolf Hitler had committed suicide together with his wife, Eva Braun. Later that day, they heard that the Minister of Propaganda, Joseph Goebbels, had also killed himself along with his wife and six children.

Franz and his family cherished that moment, when the Nazi regime finally collapsed in full. But they knew that there were still pockets of Nazi resistance on the streets, and that the war wasn't over yet.

On May 2nd, the city became eerily silent following its garrison's surrender. Radio broadcasts had also stopped. Since the Nazi regime held on to its power with the help of constant propaganda broadcasts, everyone could tell something was happening. But what? Did the war come to an end? Was the nightmare over?

Elsa got out of her hiding place together with Helmut and Kaufmann, and the three went outside to look at the street. There were no Russian soldiers in sight, but their presence was felt. Many of their neighbors were outside, fearfully looking around, fearing the Russians would pop out from an ambush at any moment.

A few days later, the entire world witnessed the Third Reich's unconditional surrender. Little by little, Germany's citizens began leaving their hiding spots, terrified. The country was in immense chaos.

Luckily for Berlin's residents, especially those who lived in the western part of town, the Americans forces set up stations where they handed out warm soup to anyone who was in need. And many, many of Berlin's residents were in need.

32

Once the war was over, it took the Berliners weeks to grasp the extent of their tragedy. They suffered from a critical shortage of food, there was no trade, and more than half the city's buildings were completely destroyed.

"Not only is this the most devastated city in the world," Franz said to Elsa and Helmut, "but it is also a city that lost its spirit and smile. It is a hopeless place to live."

Franz was tremendously worried about Karl. He hadn't heard anything from him, and had no idea where he was, or whom he could turn to in order to find out.

"It's only been a short while since the ceasefire had begun," said Erich, who by then had already become part of the family. "Nobody knows yet the full extent of what had happened or how to locate family members, now that everything is over. Also, it is unclear what will happen with the hundreds of thousands of soldiers who are now roaming the streets on their own, looking for their families."

"So what should we do?" Franz asked in desperation.

"I suggest we wait patiently until Karl sends a sign of life," Erich replied.

"If he is still alive," Helmut chimed in bitterly, immediately noticing his father and sister's terrified gazes.

Erich tried to comfort them.

"In the end, they all come home. If he is being held captive, we will know soon. The British and Americans are quite merciful. Their Prisoners of War don't just disappear."

The Kerners realized that he was being logical, and that all they could do was wait. Every day, Helmut went to check the updated list of POWs, but in vain. Karl's name wasn't on it.

But on June 15th, 1945, they realized that Erich knew what he was talking about, and that he was right to encourage them to remain patient. On that blessed day, Franz heard a knock on the door, and when he went to open it, he found both Karl and Ditmar standing there.

When he saw both of them, Franz burst into tears of joy and excitement. He felt as if his heart would explode from happiness. He had not seen his son in a year, and his brother in six months, and was so concerned he would never see them again.

"God listened to us and was graceful to us," he mumbled, as he hugged them again and again.

Ditmar told his family that after his liberation he remained in Buchenwald, so he could help the remaining inmates with contacting their families. In addition, the Anglo-American forces asked him to provide a detailed testimony regarding the Nazi crimes at the camp. Karl stayed with him the entire time, and they left together.

When they were finally free to go, the American staffers gave them new khaki clothes and fifty dollars each, for travelling. Ditmar also finally managed to shave his beard, after several months, and take a long shower. Apart from the weight he lost and general weakness, his condition was quite satisfactory.

"Why didn't you go home to see Martha and Helga?" Franz asked his brother after releasing him from another embrace.

"I am too scared they are not alive anymore," Ditmar confessed. "Could one of you accompany me there?"

They all looked at him without saying a word. Ditmar turned to Karl, and repeated his request.

"Would you be willing to join me? You've already experienced so much, you would have the strength to help me, if needed."

"Of course," Karl replied, with a tired smile.

They walked over to Oranienstrasse, where Ditmar and his family once lived. As they got closer, Ditmar's pace slowed down. He was terrified from what he might see.

"Let me have a moment to look around," he begged his nephew.

Nothing but destruction surrounded them. Ditmar looked in the direction of his home, and realized that the building was gone. He looked at Karl, his face frozen.

"You see, I told you. The house is gone. That's what I was afraid of."

"Don't jump to conclusions just yet," Karl said. "This doesn't mean anything."

They approached the spot where Ditmar's house once stood. It seemed like nothing had ever been there. With shock and fear in his eyes, Ditmar looked at all the devastated houses around. Then, a few meters away, he saw another house which, by some miracle, remained intact.

Ditmar remembered that a high-ranking government official, Joachim Wagner, lived there. He went over and knocked on the door. It was opened by an elderly woman he did not recognize.

"Excuse me, madam, are Mr. and Mrs. Wagner at home?" Ditmar asked.

"I am Mrs. Wagner's mother. Who are you, sir?"

"I am their former neighbor, Mr. Kerner. Can I speak with one of them?"

Suddenly, before the woman even had time to reply, the door opened wide and Mrs. Wagner came out, looked at him and yelled:

"Ditmar! It's you! Martha, come quick! Your husband has returned!"

Martha rushed out the door and fell into her husband's arms, weeping.

"Ditmar, where have you been when I needed you the most?

We have no home! Everything is gone." Ditmar hugged her tight.

"Where is Helga? Is she alright?"

"Don't worry, she is here, in the back yard, thank God!"

Ditmar immediately ran over to his daughter and gave her an enormous hug.

"I love you so much" he said, wiping his eyes. He took Helga's small hand and they both came back to the front of the house.

"I have to tell you everything I've gone through, but first of all, we have to find a place to live until we get back on our feet."

"Come to our home!" Karl immediately suggested. "There is enough room for everyone, and father will be happy to have you there."

Martha quickly packed the few clothes and toys they still had, and bade a tearful farewell to Mrs. Wagner and her mother.

"We will never forget what you had done for us," she said.

On their way to the Kerner's residence, Ditmar asked his wife what had happened to Mr. Wagner, their neighbor. She told him that he was killed in one of the last days of the war, while attempting to rescue people from a bombarded building.

"His death was so redundant," Martha sighed.

"Every death is redundant! You should have seen how they executed people in Buchenwald, for nothing. Human life has no value in times of war."

33

Now that he had nine people in his home, Franz felt a great responsibility towards them all, and so he decided to hold a family meeting in order to review their future possibilities.

"We must work together to organize everything we need, until some arrangement is made for the people of Berlin", he said. "It won't be easy, we've never had so many people living here at the same time, but with a little goodwill, everything will be alright."

"What do you suggest we do, father?" Elsa asked.

"First of all, I think each of you should go out and try to get some food. The shops may have something, and if not, maybe our neighbors can help. Whatever you get will be good," Franz said. "Anything is better than just sitting here at home staring at each other," added Martha.

"In that case, let's give ourselves two weeks to get organized, and then start taking care of the damages to the house," Franz concluded. "I will also go check on my pharmacy. If I can reopen, it will be a good source of income. But before we start anything, let's see how much money we have, all together."

Everyone, except for Erich, emptied their pockets. They had about 200 dollars between them all—a small fortune.

Erich was sitting quietly in the corner, looking very upset.

Franz approached him, gave him a hug and said:

"I am aware of your tragedy, but you have only two choices: either you pull yourself together and try to adapt and carry on, or you end your life the first chance you get."

"I have nothing left," the poor man began weeping. "My family and my home are gone. What is the point of living?"

"Don't give up," pleaded Franz. "You still have the most important thing: hope. Ask Ditmar about the prisoners who survived the concentration camps, then you'll understand the meaning of hope."

Erich stared into space, lost in thought.

They all got up and went to their rooms. When their door was shut, Ditmar asked Martha:

"What did you want to tell me before, when we met at the Wagners' house?"

Martha looked at him, and swallowed hard.

"I am not your wife anymore, I am a prostitute of the Russians!" she wept.

"What?!" Ditmar blurted out, stunned.

"The Russians raped me, one after the other" she said bitterly. "There were six or seven of them. they wouldn't let go until I passed out."

Ditmar tried to reach his arms towards his wife, but she slipped away from his touch.

"I became nothing more than a prostitute," she said, tears streaming down her face. "They made me do terrible things. I wanted to die. It was May 1st, I will never forget that day. Russian soldiers broke into our home and that of our neighbors. We were eight women, including Hilda Wagner. They shared us between them, like loot. They tore our bodies and souls, those barbarians..." Martha was gasping for air.

Ditmar held her tight and felt her shiver in shame and pain. He began sobbing as well. He stroked her hair and tried to soothe her, but was not very successful. What she went through was too difficult for both of them to bear.

"No husband, no home, no honor," Martha continued, in between sobs. "I wanted to kill myself, the only reason I didn't was my concern for Helga. Luckily, I had Hilda Wagner on my side. A strong woman, without whom I would have been dead by now."

"I understand, my love, please try to put this behind you," Ditmar said.

"How can you call me 'my love'? I am defiled!"

"You are my eternal love," Ditmar said softly. "You survived being raped, and I survived Buchenwald. Not to compare our experiences, but mine was also horrible."

That was the first time Martha heard Ditmar speak of the concentration camp. She stopped crying and looked at him.

"It won't be easy, but we'll get through this together," Ditmar added. "Tell me, did you get your period this month?"

"It's too early, it's not due for another couple of weeks. I hope to God I'm not pregnant from those animals!" cried Martha.

"I am so full of hatred towards this damned regime for everything it had put us through!" Ditmar said in a fury. "And not just us, but the entire German nation. I'm sure that hundreds of thousands, millions perhaps, feel the same."

That night at the dinner table, as the candle lights cast shadows on their faces, Franz said in earnest:

"I don't know what will happen here in a month, a year or ten years. In the 1920s, I married a Jewish girl and we had three children, and until recently, no one knew that Jewish blood was running through their veins. We suffered just like all of the other loyal German citizens. And yet, had I been given the chance to relive my life, I would have married the same beautiful Jewish girl, my Marlene."

Elsa got up and kissed him.

"Thank you, father, for what you have just said."

Now it was Karl's turn to speak. "We have to acknowledge the fact that we are Jewish, to be even proud of it. Only one group underwent such incomprehensible horrors and suffering during the six years of war—the Jewish people. I don't know how many Jews were murdered, but it must have been over three million. And I am intentionally using the word 'murdered', rather than killed. When I was on the Polish Front in 1941, I heard that Poland's entire Jewish community was either exiled or annihilated."

Everyone in the room looked at each other, shocked.

"I had friends in my unit who were killed in a war that everyone wanted," Karl continued. "The crime of the German people is that we believed everything we were told, and fervently accepted Hitler's promises: independence, strengthening the army, bolstering the economy, Nazi bliss for all! But I faced death a thousand times! I saw the dead, whose blood is now calling us from the ground: 'Why? What for?'"

"Until now, I had no idea that my brother's wife was Jewish," Ditmar suddenly said. "This is a big surprise. I'm glad you kept this a secret from me. I don't know what I might have done, had I known this before. I was the most submissive servant of the regime."

"You wouldn't have dared turn me in," Franz replied.

"I can't tell you that," Ditmar replied honestly. "You must remember that I was active in looting Jewish property all over

Germany. I remember one night, after the defeat in Stalingrad in February 1943. The top SS generals were looking for a good reason to celebrate, so we were all invited to meet Himmler in a luxurious hall in Berlin. There was so much alcohol there, and we all drank ourselves into a stupor.

"At some point, Himmler asked Dr. Fink how many impure Aryans were employed in the German industry. Fink replied that the number most likely exceeded three million, mostly Russians and Poles. Under the influence of the alcohol, Himmler screamed in fury: 'We have been working for years to expel a quarter of a million Jews from Germany, and now I hear that you have been contaminating our land with those filthy Slaves, that inferior race?!'"

Ditmar continued his story. "Fink responded that those were Göring's instructions, in order to boost the industrial effort, as almost all of the German workers were drafted. Himmler turned red with rage. When he calmed down a little, he said something that characterized the type of solutions favored by the Nazis:

'We will have to eliminate them, but not before they will have completed their tasks.'"

The family gazed at Ditmar, who went on.

"The lies and hypocrisy of the Nazi leaders, towards one another and all of Germany, were truly unbelievable. They did not utter a single word of truth, only lies and more lies. They betrayed each other, until finally they betrayed their leader, Himmler, who then betrayed Hitler. And the Führer, who did he betray? Our people! This is a historical lesson for the generations to come. It is too late for any of us here."

***

Towards the end of 1945, Helmut was feeling restless, and decided to travel through Europe on a quest for answers, justice and self-enlightenment. His journey mirrored that of Diogenes, a Greek philosopher from the 4th century BC, who despised the wealth and injustice that prevailed around him, and moved from one place to another with a torch in his hands, searching for justice—which he never found. Helmut did not return home until 1947.

By that time, Franz had reopened his pharmacy, and Karl was married to Eva, his high-school sweetheart: he fulfilled the promise he had given her during their last meeting in Saarbrücken, and found her after the war. She was trying to survive, all alone, in her family home, which was left in shambles after an air raid which killed her parents. She and Karl built a new home and a new life for themselves in the western part of Berlin.

Elsa had moved to the eastern part of town, to put her Russian to good use by working at a local hospital. The connection with her was eventually lost.

Helmut remained restless. He wasn't able to forget the immense pain he saw on the faces of those few surviving European Jews, and kept thinking about their stories. He told his father that he can no longer live in Germany after what his people—or rather, those he believed to be his people—had done to the Jews. He had developed an identification not only with the Jewish people, but also with the Zionist cause.

In December 1947, Helmut traveled to Italy, where he boarded the illegal immigration ship "Maria Christina". The ship sailed to Palestine with more than 800 hopeful immigrants from Romania, Poland and Hungary. However, British Mandate forces

seized the ship, and deported its passengers to a detention camp in Cyprus.

Helmut, however, somehow made it to his destination, and fought in Israel's War of Independence in 1948. That was the last time anyone had ever heard of him. His traces were lost during the war. His destiny remains a mystery.

The once tight-knit Kerner family shattered into a thousand small fragments, just like the broken glass of that fateful *Kristallnacht* of 1938.

Epilogue

Like many political science professors, historians, statesmen, journalists and authors before me, I have also tried to analyze the tragedy that befell Europe during the dark period of the Nazi reign, first over Germany and then over most of the continent. I hope that my quest was at least partially successful. It is quite difficult to provide a rational justification as to how Nazism ruled Europe, given the deep hatred and evil that characterized it.

The Nazi ideology was based on three principles:

A. *Rassentheorien* (race theories): opinions and beliefs regarding the existence of certain traits as belonging only to a certain race of people. Based on this, the Nazism created a hierarchal method of measuring the essence and quality of each race in civilization. Hitler believed that the Aryan-German-Christians were the "master race", the purest and most superior. The Slavic race was inferior to that "master race" and, according to Nazi ideology, could be enslaved, expelled and even exterminated. The Jewish race was at the very bottom of the hierarchy, a "sub-race" that must be exterminated.

B. *Lebensraum* (habitat): this was the ideological justification for Germany's need for territorial expansion (or rather, invasion) into Central and Eastern Europe. Hitler wanted to expel some 30 million Slavs beyond the Ural Mountains, and provide the "master race" with the vacated territory. Fortunately for the Russians, that plan was never realized.

C. *Führerprinzip* (the leader principle): the belief that the leader is the sole authority regarding all important state decisions. Therefore, all civilians must obey him and sacrifice themselves for the purpose of achieving his goals. This belief fueled Hitler's cult of personality.

The Germans adopted those principles enthusiastically, because they went hand-in-hand with the obliteration of the Treaty of Versailles, imposed on them following the First World War. Germany was stripped from its dignity and had to pay enormous reparations to the victorious countries. This was a heavy burden on the everyday life of its citizens, as well as on the nation's morale.

Hitler appointed 500 of his most loyal, obedient men, for senior positions in his regime. They believed that the Third Reich should take over most of Europe by means of war. In his manifesto, *Mein Kampf* (My Struggle), Hitler explicitly stated that "Germany's problems can only be solved through force". This "force" was to be used against those he considered as enemies of the regime: Jews, communists, socialists, liberals, the Slavic nations, homosexuals, the sick and elderly, the Anglo- Americans. In short—most of the world.

In the Nazi regime itself, violence was considered a superior value. At its core was the physical elimination of any and all regime opponents.

Europe emerged from the First World War victorious, but weakened. The nations' top concern was improving the working class' standard of living. In 1932, Field Marshal Paul von Hindenburg was elected president by 19 million Germans. Hitler, his opponent, gained only 13 million votes. But only a year later, following great political unrest and instability, Hindenburg appointed Hitler as chancellor, paving the way for the rise of Nazism.

In 1935, Hitler proclaimed general, immediate and mandatory military conscription in Germany. This law violated the Treaty of Versailles, which stated that Germany was not permitted to have an army of more than 100 thousand men. France and England protested feebly, without taking any concrete action. By 1936, Hitler cancelled the Treaty altogether, and the German army took over the Ruhr.

While Germany was taking over areas and countries throughout the continent, Europe as a whole still lived in its pipe dream of a good, peaceful life, without war and violence. Germany's political and diplomatic terror eventually led to six years of a horrific war, and to the deaths of millions of innocent civilians.

Among those who perished were 20 million Russians, 10 million Germans, 5.5 million Poles, and another 10 million from the other European and North African countries. And of course—6 million Jews, one third of the world's entire Jewish population. Over 40 million were wounded, and countless others were displaced.

***

In 1938, an anti-Jewish pogrom, known as *Kristallnacht* (Night of Broken/Shattered Glass), took place throughout Germany. It symbolized the peak of many tragic, anti-Semitic events that had been carried out against the nation's Jewish population. Those events led Ze'ev Jabotinsky, the Zionist leader, to call on Poland's

Jews to leave everything behind and immigrate to Palestine. However, most of them refused to leave their comfortable lives and remained in Poland, oblivious to the tragedy that would soon befall them.

In 1939, Nazi Germany invaded Poland and began the systematic annihilation of the Jewish people. The Jews were slayed without mercy, and with little resistance.

The Nuremberg Trials didn't fully even the score with the Nazi leaders. However, the sparks of *Kristallnacht* transformed into sparks of hope for the Jewish people, who in 1948 established the State of Israel as a will and testament of those six million who perished in the Holocaust.

The establishment of Israel corrected a great historical wrong. However, the price the Jewish nation had to pay for its own homeland was too great and horrific to comprehend.

Today, only sixty years since the conclusion of that dark chapter in the history of mankind, millions of young people have never heard of it. In history classes around the world, the Holocaust is often omitted from the curriculum.

Therefore, I decided to write this book as both a reminder and a warning: those who do not learn history are doomed to repeat it. The future generations must carry World War II and the Holocaust as part of their collective memory, thereby making sure that such atrocities will never happen again.

Baruch Cohen
Eve of Holocaust Remembrance Day
2006

The Decade of Tears

by Baruch (Boby) Cohen

In May 1940, Europe was not yet in flames. However, the whole of Western Europe, except for Great Britain, had fallen into the hands of Hitler. The actual outburst would start only a year later, after the Nazis' invasion of the USSR.

The first book of Baruch (Boby) Cohen, which has been scheduled for publication in 2021, is a historical novel that recounts the independent struggle of three strong-willed Jewish men from different parts of the globe during WW2, which Cohen termed as "The Decade of Tears".

In their fight for survival, Benny, Alex and Ronny, witnessed the Germans' glorious victories, their great losses and finally the collapse of the Third Reich. They found themselves in a displaced camp in Cyprus intended for Jewish Holocaust survivors, where they connected for a common goal: to reach the State of Israel, the newly-established Jewish state.

Together, they escaped the camp, despite the British tough guard, and illegally arrived to the forming Jewish state, where they joined Israel Defense Forces and fought in the War of Independence.

The Decade of Tears is a historical document, depicting the suffering and pains of Jewish communities in Romania, France, and Italy, the birthplace of our heroes, who aimed to escape to the only sanctuary they had. Most others were not as fortunate.

Milton Keynes UK
Ingram Content Group UK Ltd.
UKHW020806170524
442760UK00002B/20